Exposing Atalanta

An Enemies to Lovers Romantic Suspense
Suspense

Molly Briar

To the redhaired hunk I married

CONTENTS

Author's Note

This book features disturbing content, to include murder, staged suicide and drug overdoses of non-main characters, graphic, spicy sexual content and other things that would be typical of a book about assassins.

I am also well aware that travel nursing is not accurately depicted in this fictional world. I ask the audience, and the many wonderful nurses out there, to please suspend their disbelief so that the story can happen.

PROLOGUE

It's show time.

Ivan Leclerc thrashed, sputtered, and struggled for air in the frigid water. I pressed harder on the back of his neck. Briefly, I empathized with him as he fought for air. I'm no fan of aquatic endeavors myself, but fuck him—he made his choices, and now, he'll die because of them.

Swans sailed gracefully across the clear, cold, sky, darts of alabaster feathers shimmering in the moonlight. To the east, the island castle of Chateau de Chillon loomed like a mythical fortress guarding the gate to the pristine alps.

Thirty seconds had passed.

Surely, he hadn't expected this when I ushered him down the mansion's stone steps. He came willingly, giggling as he staggered toward the lake in an inebriated haze. He was still oblivious when I dropped him on the rocky shore.

Until I submerged his arrogant, privileged ass in the lake, he had no reason to fear for his life. After all, what could go wrong at an exclusive charity gala in one of the most expensive countries in the world? The help, like me, was never a threat to men like him.

One minute.

He continued to struggle, flailing his arms in the icy water, alternating between attempting to pull me down and push me away. He was nearly twice my weight, and half a foot taller. If not for the drug I'd slipped into his expensive vodka tonic, it would be my lungs filling with Swiss lake water.

As he thrashed, I applied more weight to his head. I extended my arms, thrusting my head and shoulders back, staring upward to the sky. The stars were bright and twinkling. Small, silver clouds drifted lazily overhead. The lake and distant snow-capped mountains resembled something out of a fairytale. Not a bad place to shuffle off the mortal coil.

One Minute, thirty seconds.

All things considered, there were worse ways to go. In fact, I read somewhere that drowning is one of the more pleasant ways. Those who have been resuscitated reported a feeling of euphoria and peace before everything went black. I hope I never confirm that.

He finally stopped struggling; the bubbles floating up with his screams slowed. He was surrendering to the inevitable end.

One minute, forty-five seconds.

I pushed him into the lake, his body floated peacefully in the waves that beat on the shore. He was just another cautionary tale of alcohol and large bodies of water.

Two minutes. See you in hell, Ivan Leclerc.

Time to head back inside for the toasts.

CHAPTER ONE

Montreux, Switzerland

"Your contributions save thousands of lives each year." His cultivated American voice was earnest; his blue eyes genuine and kind as he stared out at the grand ballroom from the large projected screen on the white wall.

An amicable face, wind-swept and sunburned, smiled down on the crowd from a large screen propped on a small stage built for this occasion. His blue eyes glinted in the harsh sun.

"Thank you for your ongoing support." Alexander Baas, tech mogul and messiah to many continued to say. A dozen Baas Medical Staff in white medical scrubs stood beneath the screen, as rigid as statues. "I apologize. I cannot be with you this evening, but many of my wonderful staff will be there, ready to accept your generosity and answer any questions you may have." He flashed that winning smile and the video's triumphal music crescendoed. "Again, thank you for all you have given us and remember, those who have the most must give the most."

The video faded, and I was relieved that the show was over.

The lights brightened. Guests clapped politely with their drinks in hand and the orchestra resumed a waltz.

Uniformed Baas Medical personnel carrying wooden baskets worked the room, collecting envelope donations and freshly signed cheques from well-dressed patrons.

Ivan Leclerc, an acquaintance from my Oxford days, chuckled wryly, swirling his double vodka-tonic before taking an obscene gulp of the overpriced potato-water. He was, as usual, feeling superior. When he was rat-arsed, he fancied himself quite the clever chap. And tonight, he was right and plenty rat-arsed. He turned toward me, his wide, red face contorted into a smirk. His stomach was too tight for his Kiton Blue Blazer. It was barely hanging on by the seams. He was also too short for the cut, but that was no matter. I would, as a good Oxford mate should, humor his dickless musings.

He shook his head in disbelief. "You St. Michael's kids…" he began, his nasal, royal voice dribbled with pompous arrogance.

He was referring to the alumni of our boarding school, St. Michael's. The campus was barely a stone's throw from where we stood.

I was here at the behest of my former classmate, Alexander Baas, founder, and CEO of Baas Medical Technologies. The man of the hour, whose face had just graced the large screen. He was a renowned philanthropist, funding clinics and bringing medical aid to the most underserved populations. Ivan was the kind of twat who scoffed at that kind of thing, preferring to believe that his inherited wealth was a sign of merit.

"We like to call ourselves chocolatiers," I off-handedly remarked, gesturing slightly with my whiskey tumbler.

"You're all so loyal to one another." He was mocking us. "It's inane."

I ignored his last insult and simply shrugged my shoulders. "Chocolate is thicker than blood, old man."

"Ah, your silly little sayings." Ivan dismissed with a wave of his plump hand, before pointing at me, his finger right in my face. "You're the worst of them."

"How so?" I inquired, with a lazy, quirked brow. *Oh, please, give us your wisdom, you shit-faced little weasel.*

I never liked Ivan. He always had an ax to grind and disliked everyone and everything. He was very unpleasant all around, but politeness and a shared university dictated that I extend him a little courtesy.

It was useless to be offended by gnats like Ivan "The knob" Leclerc.

"You're daft enough to believe this ruse." He chuckled, his hand gesturing to where the screen had been. "Do you really think that Baas believes in this charity malarkey? Year after year, we donate millions to these plebs. Then, year after year, we donate even more." He was slurring, his drink spilling with his gesticulations.

"They don't want to change, and we don't want them to change. It's the natural order of things. And your friend there," He casually waved his hand at the screen again. "He's a fucking genius and has you all eating his arse." He chuckled and stumbled away, bracing on the walls to steady himself.

A platinum blonde Baas Medical staff member came to his aid, grabbing his arm and leading him out of the ballroom before he could make a bigger spectacle of himself.

"A dance?" said a woman's melodic voice.

I knew that voice. My fiancée. The woman I'd known long before she became the quintessential "it" girl. The awkward lass I once knew was now a fashion icon, a household name, and occupying more and more of my thoughts. But not in the good way. Not a way that I could tolerate.

"As you wish, Pippa," I tried not to let my irritation show as she took my hand, twirling herself beneath my arm. Her custom red Valentino dress swirled effortlessly about her as she moved with the grace of a ballerina.

"I think the Maldives for our honeymoon." Her voice sounded like silver, clinking on crystal stemware. Her voice dripped of money from the finest British pedigree. "And maybe we could settle on the Riviera for our permanent home." She glided through the dance floor, barely needing me to lead. "What do you think?"

"That sounds fine, Pippa." I responded flatly. The orchestra's instrumental rendition of Sondheim's *Being Alive* carried us across the floor.

It didn't sound fine. I hated the beach; I despised the heat. If I never had to step foot on sand ever again, it would still be too soon. But she didn't know any of this. If she did, she didn't care.

"Just fine?" Her perfect face soured. Her frown deepened. "We've been engaged for five years. Don't you think it's time we set a date?"

She stopped dancing and smacked me on the chest and pushed me away with her left hand. The one with a five-carat solitaire diamond on a slim, French manicured finger.

"Why now?" I placed my hands in my pocket. I did not intend to have this conversation here, but it was as good a place as any.

"Why can't you commit to this?" She sounded desperate. "Why can't you commit to us?"

My shoulders slumped, and I ran a hand over my face and beard.

I had a plan. I was going to take her to a private dinner and steer the conversation to our many differences. I would let her know how we were incompatible. I would get her to admit that she was as numb and bored by this whole thing as I was... but she was forcing my hand in a ballroom, with press and paparazzi meandering around.

Maybe she won't cause a scene with this kind of audience.

"Pippa..." I said in a low, soothing tone. "There's no rush..."

"It won't work this time." She crossed her arms and stamped her Louboutin heel. "I want to set a date. It's been five bloody years!"

I took a fortifying breath. It was time to be cold, and to harden myself for the task ahead. We needed to end this. *I* needed to end this.

If it broke her heart, so be it.

We had been trapped in this for too long, and we weren't getting any younger. Nor were we growing in love.

"I hate the Maldives." My voice stayed calm, not giving away my concealed agitation. "I hate the beach. You and I have been a terrible match from the beginning."

She placed a hand on her chest as though my words insulted her.

"I have always preferred the cold, the mountains, and my home is the Highlands." I looked at the pointed toe on her shoe, then ran my hand through my hair. "And we've known that we're not a good pair. We knew it in school. We know it now. Isn't it time to end this charade?"

Her angelic face changed, transforming into one of malice.

Ah, there it is. The Machiavellian princess under her facade.

"You're obviously having a mid-life crisis." She looked down at the ring on her hand as it sparkled in the lamp lights. "You'd be crazy to call us off." She looked up at me, raising her brow.

I was. I knew it too. She was perfect on paper. A model, the daughter of a shipping magnate, and one of the most desirable women in the world. Yet, in over thirty years of knowing each other, we had never once seen eye to eye.

"You're right." I shrugged. "But I haven't been happy. Neither have you."

"Are you being noble?" she said, her eyes squinting and suspicious.

"No, Pippa. I'm being selfish." I turned away from her. I tried to remain neutral but couldn't help a slight agitation in my voice. "There's got to be something better out there."

"Fine, if you need some more time, then... fine." She raised one manicured eyebrow, completely unconvinced. "I'm tired of this, Callum. I really am. When you come crawling back, I'll be expecting an upgrade." She flashed me her already enormous ring.

She put a hand on her jutted hip and pursed her lips before flipping her hair and strutting away from me with that seductive runway walk.

It could have gone worse, I thought with relief.

Her overall indifference told me that I had done the right thing.

Shrugging, I stepped out into the cool air of the marble balcony. The night was gorgeous. The balcony was quiet. A waiter stood at the empty bar, a linen napkin over one arm as he scrubbed the tabletop. I leaned an elbow on the bar and looked at the placid lake and the snow-capped peaks in the distance. The landscape was dotted with little towns, and a lazy train chugged along the shoreline.

"Give me another," I said, dropping my glass on the bar. I placed my face in my hands and groaned. When I emerged, I looked at the bartender. Except it wasn't the bartender at all. It was a little woman with platinum pixie hair and a deep brown tan. Her lips were thick and naturally plump in contrast to a small, flat nose and almond-shaped brown eyes as dark as the most fertile earth.

She was dressed in white Baas Medical scrubs, a donation basket discarded on the bar, filled to the brim with enveloped cheques. Her eyes were narrow and amused. There was something in the tautness of her skin that hinted at a level of fitness that was uncommon in women.

It was fascinating.

"I'm dreadfully sorry." I shook off my stupor. "I thought the other chap was still here."

"No worries," she said, her voice high, dry, and American. She didn't smile at me, but reached for a tulip glass, making herself comfortable at the unattended bar. "To the top 0.1 percent, all of us plebs look the same."

She had clearly overheard Ivan's snobbish remarks.

"That's not true at all." I chuckled, wanting to distance myself from imps like him. "I simply have a lot on my mind."

She poured a generous amount. Far more than what the bartender would have. Her audacity was charming.

"You're American." I stated.

"Is it obvious?" She shrugged. "Do you people still call us the colonies?"

"I'm Scottish, love," I said, playing up a Scottish brogue. I took a sip of the Macallan and basked in the scent. "So, not quite the same."

"So, what's on your mind, champ? Did someone scuff your expensive shoes?" There was a teasing glint in her eye. "Did the maid forget to dust your favorite polo trophy? That must be hard. Gadzooks, m'lord! Tis a travesty!" She mocked a pompous British accent.

I smiled at her. She smiled back.

Her audacity should offend me, but her smile made me pause. She was lovely, though a little plain in her white scrubs.

"Have a drink with me, and I'll tell you." I leaned on the bar and challenged her.

"Yeah?" She was goading me. I liked it.

"Yeah." I mocked her American, almost valley girl, voice.

She grabbed a glass and poured a serving for herself. She drank it in one gulp. That was both impressive and a little appalling. But I didn't comment.

"I am recently single." I admitted in a stage whisper, giving her a mock toast with my whiskey. "After five years of being engaged."

"Five... *years*?" Her eyes grew wide in shock. "Shit or get off the pot, dude."

"Indeed." I brought the whiskey to my lips to stifle a laugh. "What a charming expression."

"So, what kept you from committing? Is she hideous?" She whispered the last part like we were conspirators, bringing our heads together into a tête-à-tête. "Pustules and warts. Maybe a club foot, or a hairy mole? A humpback? Is she here?"

She excitedly looked around, glancing at the swirl of ball gowns in the great hall.

I laughed. It was a genuine laugh that bubbled from deep in my gut. Pippa could never make me laugh like this. Was this what I had been missing? There was chemistry in the air between us, and it seeped under my skin.

"Look for yourself." I nodded to the dance floor. "She's the strawberry blonde in red."

The girl looked at the dance floor, and her mouth hung open. She looked at me, then at Pippa, then back at me.

"Are you gay?" she whispered. "My gaydar didn't go off… I mean… is that why…?"

I laughed again. "No, straight as the day is 24 hours."

I looked her up and down. The boxy white Bass Medical uniform scrubs didn't do her petite body any justice. But she didn't need any glitter to shine. She was beautiful. Not in the way that might stop a man dead in his tracks. But in the way that demanded your attention. It insisted on your constant study.

"So, what is it? Does she have bad breath in the morning?" She was teasing again. "Does she sweat when it's warm? Are her hands cold in winter? What sin has she committed?"

"We're just not compatible." I tried to seem nonchalant, but I cared a great deal about what this woman thought.

"Boss, there is no man in the world that isn't compatible with that Aphrodite." She was laughing at my expense, but it didn't hurt me. I enjoyed seeing her laugh. "It sure sounds like you're the problem."

"What if I don't want an Aphrodite?" I admitted. "What if I want an Atalanta?"

"Atalanta." She said the name as though she could taste it. "Hmm." She looked pensive. "I think she's a big flight risk, don't you? Bit of a runaway bride." She grinned. "Do you have a storage of golden apples hidden somewhere?"

Of course, she knew who Atalanta was.

The Greek myth of a woman raised in the wild. Her father wanted to arrange her marriage. Her stipulation was that she would only marry the man who could beat her in a foot race. She was faster than anyone alive. A suitor asked the gods for help. He was given three golden apples. Each time she was about to beat him, he would throw out an irresistible apple. Atalanta was distracted, and she'd slow down to pick it up. He did that three times, thus winning the race, and her hand.

Everything about this encounter felt like fate. I watched her natural, full lips touch the rim of her glass; the liquid kissed their plumpness. I felt my blood heat at the thought of tasting that whiskey on her lips and fought the urge to lean in and do just that.

"What about you?" I coughed to pull myself from her spell. "What does your man think of you being out here, getting a random man drunk?"

The liquor was getting to my head. Being in the company of a witty woman was the most glorious of pastimes.

"No man." She smiled and offered no other information.

"*Quel dommage!*" I exclaimed the French phrase theatrically. *What a pity!* "Maybe you're the real Atalanta."

She leaned on the bar and raised her brow in a silent question.

She smelled like a tropical flower, sweet and musky. I didn't know if the scent was in her hair or on her skin. To grab her by the neck and pull her in and run my nose over her throat would be untoward, but the urge was unbelievable.

I resolved to see her again. I was about to ask for her name when I heard Pippa stomping loudly to the banister of the balcony. She leaned a slender elbow on it and looked at me, her eyes narrowed. She gave one judgmental look at the girl before looking out into the lake.

Her hand trembled over her open mouth and her long finger pointed down to the edge of the water. Then she screamed.

I leaned over the railing to look.

I recognized the Kiton blue blazer before I recognized the man in them. It bobbed lifelessly in the shallow waves as swans gracefully floated nearby.

I leapt from the railing, landing on the nearby grass. I dove into the water, my dress shoes slipping on the rocks. I clutched Ivan's jacket and hauled him onto the rocky shore, twisting him onto his back.

I felt for a pulse. There was none. It was far too late.

He was blue, and long gone. I looked up. Pippa was still screaming.

A small, stoic face peered down at me. It was the woman behind the bar, her skin dark in contrast to the white scrubs and platinum hair.

She stood motionless, staring calmly at the spectacle. Others around her looked on in shock and panic. Our eyes locked briefly.

What did that little minx know?

Then she turned and disappeared from view.

CHAPTER TWO

The view of the Thames dominated the 35th floor office through spotless floor-to-ceiling windows. The flawlessly adorned room contained millions of dollars of contemporary furnishings and art. An art déco wooden desk embossed with golden lines to emphasize its exquisitely crafted angles held court at one end of the room. A red Afghan rug, intricately woven with patterns comprised of gold and silver threads, covered the expansive floor space. It wouldn't surprise me if the threads were made of actual gold and silver. Despite the extravagance, the real showstopper was the view of the water weaving by the famous London Eye.

I'd been here many times before, but the sights just beyond those windows always left me in awe. Almost as much as the office's occupant, Rashid Khan.

Rashid stood a few feet from me, gazing out the window, swirling a Macallan single-malt Scotch in his large palm. Across the river was a pristine building of glass, crowned with a blue logo made up of lines of latitude and longitude on an empty globe. In the middle of that circle was a blue caduceus with the letters B, T and M. It was the symbol of Baas Tech Medical, owned by Alexander Baas, my old classmate. Rashid and Alex were competitors, and between the two of them, they controlled almost all medical manufacturing in the western world.

This view was proper London, like the accent I cultivated for business.

A large ice ball tinkled against Rashid's glass, the sound of it like nails on a chalkboard.

I took my whiskey neat, as God had intended.

But our method of taking whiskey was only one of many striking differences between us.

His suit fit him perfectly. Was it Brioni? Desmond Marrion? No, even a cursory inspection of the cut, the seams or the gold and red flourish on the lapel told the tale. This was custom — one of a kind, and why not? Men like Rashid always had a tailor on call. There was never a hair out of place on his thick, black curly mane. There was never a blemish on that perfect, deeply tanned skin. I imagined him like the king of Versailles, with courtiers waiting on him from the moment he opened his eyes, scrubbing him with pumice stones and massaging him with expensive oils.

On his wrist hung an Acheron Constantine Tour de L'ille, a modest $1.5 million watch for the discerning magnate.

I looked down at my own Rolex Sea-Dweller and smiled. My old boarding school motto "Levavi Oculus", Latin for *I will lift up my eyes*, was engraved around the watch face. I was practically a pauper in the face of Rashid Khan's billions, but I liked the man. Rashid was a level-headed and, sometimes, even relatable multi-billionaire. Or was he in the trillions?

The man won't look down on you for not having a Cesare Attolini shirt. If you came in wearing a thrift store suit, he wouldn't notice. But he'd notice if that suit was wrinkled. He didn't have issues with people on a budget, but he hated it when someone lacked attention to detail.

He was my kind of man.

So it was a complete mystery how this titan of industry could have spawned a complete twat for a son.

"Junior is..." Rashid lamented in his perfect British English, "challenged."

He took a sip, and I followed. It was spectacular. I smelled the sherry cask, hints of oranges and pears before I tasted the well-balanced, spicy burn. Then the hint of caramel and honey lingered on the tongue and in the nostrils. As I tilted the tumbler, I saw how the liquid creeped back down, clinging to the glass in a thick trail before settling at the bottom. That long leg was a sign that this beauty was 25 years old. This was, by far, my favorite scent. If they ever created a Macallan cologne, I would bathe in it.

"It can't be easy," I said, not because I believed it, but because I needed to say something to move the conversation forward. I wasn't just here to enjoy a good single-malt, though that was worth the trip.

"No. No, it isn't," Rashid continued. "I thought I gave him the world. We sent him to the best boarding schools with those silly knee-high wool socks and pleated shorts."

I hid my smile behind my glass. I had attended those same schools.

"And those stupid blazers and neck ties. But he probably just needed some attention. We didn't know how to do that for him." Rashid went behind his desk and sat down in the leather, ergonomic chair.

It was subtle, but I noted that the expensive brown leather shoes had orthopedic soles. Rashid was showing signs of aging. That was a surprise. I never really thought guys like Rashid aged like normal people. Did his back hurt when he got out of bed? Did Rashid feel exhausted even after a decent night's sleep on his expensive, and probably enormous, bed? Did he crave afternoon naps?

"I need to make a man out of Junior," said Rashid. "He must participate in the business. He must show his face and stop gallivanting around. How will he take his rightful place in the company? I hope that this trip to Argentina will show him how lucky he is, and how good he has it. Maybe it will show him that he has a greater duty to the world than just partying and girls."

He said the last word with incredible disdain, as if "girls" were the greatest of all evils.

"Not every man can have a childhood sweetheart." I chuckled behind my glass. "Many of us have to sow our wild oats."

The first woman Rashid Khan ever loved was the woman he married, and they were bound for life. Not only were the two of them perfect together, but she was a high-powered lawyer. They were two careerists in a marriage of complete and total understanding. I envied it. I hoped for something that looked a little more romantic, but at 37 years old, I suspected I was in for a lifetime of bachelorhood.

Rashid wiped his face with his palm and released a sigh of exasperation. He placed his glass down on the desk and pressed a button on the black phone speaker.

"Dieter, come in here," he said, before turning off the intercom.

"He can learn," I reassured Rashid with an indulgent smile. "He'll grow out of it. Many children who have the misfortune of being born rich do."

"Like you?" Rashid grinned at me with a raised brow.

"Like me." I shrugged.

"What helped you become a man?" Rashid's smile faded, and he was genuinely curious. "What kept you from spending your parents' money?"

"Honestly, I don't think I can really advise you." I put my glass down on his desk. I'd have to tread carefully. "The wealth I grew up with and the wealth that Junior grew up with are worlds apart. I knew I would have to work. Our estates don't make enough to sustain themselves, much less a life of luxury. The MacLachlans are better off than most, but we're nothing compared to the Khans."

I picked up my glass again and toasted to him. He smiled at the compliment and raised his glass in return.

Rashid became pensive again, staring out into space.

The door opened, and in strode a blond-haired, square jawed man in a suit. He was going gray at the temples. His eyes were the color of ice. An earpiece dangled on his shoulder, and I noted the bulge of a pistol under his jacket.

He marched; he didn't walk. His shoulders were square, and his movements had a certain cadence to it. He was clearly a military man. Maybe a mercenary?

"Callum," Rashid flicked his hand at the newcomer. "Have you met Dieter Müller, my head of security?"

"I haven't had the pleasure." I rose from my seat and stretched my hand. "Is that a German or Swiss name?"

He firmly shook it, then stepped away, eyeing me from head to toe. I did the same.

"Swiss, of course." His light Alamance accent, a Germanic Swiss language, was flat, with a hint of irritation. His pronunciation was mostly British, but I could hear a trace of something else there. Something eastern European. It was very slight, only recognizable because I honed my radar with a misspent youth in an international school.

I'd be offended by his rigid demeanor, but I grew up in Montreux. The man was just being Swiss. As kids, we circulated a book entitled "A Comprehensive list of Swiss Jokes." The pages were blank.

"Of course." I, a proud Scot, also reverted to British English when brokering deals, so his own British-English was just par for the course. It gave people the impression of professionalism and intelligence.

No one wanted to sound American.

I kept my Scottish voice in my back pocket for only my closest allies. It may not appear the most sophisticated, but as far as I was concerned, it was the most masculine.

And I know many lassies agree with that.

Müller and I sized each other up. If we were roosters, we'd be scratching our talons into on the ground, circling, and flapping our feathers. I noted his suit and recognized it as Hugo Boss. Not a surprising choice for his profession.

"I am familiar with your illustrious reputation, of course," Müller supplied without a hint of emotion. Not revealing if that was a good or bad thing. Again, that was very Swiss of him.

"You have the advantage then, I'm afraid." The statement was an invitation for Müller to supply his own resume and background, but the stoic man didn't respond.

Well, that's interesting.

Most men would give an elevator speech, talking themselves up in fifty words or less. Not him, though. Maybe it's because he's Swiss. They were a race held together by their economy. Maybe that frugality extended to his conversation as well. Either that, or he was used to keeping secrets.

The posturing was over. I wasn't sure who ended up on top of that little exchange, but I was about two inches taller than him, so I'd called that a win for me. We turned back to Rashid, waiting for the purpose of this introduction.

"I am sending Junior to Argentina, as you both know." Rashid picked up his whiskey again and downed what was left in the glass. "But I have had concerns since the last time I let him fly out of the nest."

My eyebrow rose in question. Rashid didn't answer, but instead nodded to Müller, inviting him to speak.

"He suffered an overdose." Müller supplied after an awkward pause. "It was heroin and hallucinogens."

"Oh?" I supplied, simply to acknowledge the new information. I gave Müller a little nod, to try to prompt him to continue his explanation, because I still wasn't connecting any dots. He exhaled through his nose, his chest rising and falling with the effort. He may as well have rolled his eyes at the inconvenience of my ignorance.

I was beginning to enjoy his exasperation.

"He was partying in Ibiza." Müller turned to his boss and frowned. "He was found in his room hallucinating and seizing. If the maid hadn't come in for their daily cleaning, and the paramedics alerted just a few seconds later, Junior would be dead."

I was still missing whatever point was being made.

"That is unfortunate, but I don't think that's really a security concern." It was a statement, but my voice had an interrogative inflection. "Maybe rehab, or a clinic would be more suited for this sort of..." I grasped for the correct word to use, but then decided to follow Rashid's lead. "Challenge."

Rashid and Müller shared a look. Müller took a seat, and I followed suit. We both faced toward Rashid, who reclined in his leather chair behind his great desk and cleared his throat.

"I am neither blind nor stupid. I know my son has vices." He let out his own sigh of disappointment. "But until that day, heroin was not one of them. My son is a drunk, a 'pot-head' as they say." The old man's cheeks went red, his lips curling in disgust at the colloquialism. "He has partaken of some of the stupidity that plagues his generation. Ayahuasca, mescaline, hallucinogens while sitting in a hot tent in the middle of the American desert all for the purposes of *finding themselves* while dancing in hippie clothes." His nose crinkled, and his face comically frowned like the words tasted sour on his tongue.

Rashid seemed truly old. He got up from his seat and looked at foggy old London as a gray cloud reflected into the even grayer water of the Thames. He took in a fortifying breath before continuing.

"He has a weakness for women. But until that day, he had never been the type to use heroin."

I was skeptical. In that long list of vices, it did not seem like heroin was far from the realm of possibility. But I didn't say anything. Rashid was one of my better paying clients. Any special security needs, big speeches, special events... the man paid out the nose. Even the consultation fee for this meeting kept the lights on at Caledonia Security.

Rashid let out a deep, sardonic chuckle before turning back to me. His deep, black eyes almost pleading for a little grace, and a lot of understanding.

"I know what you are thinking, Callum." He went to the glass bar and poured himself another drink. "You are thinking that I am a father who loves his son and cannot believe that he might overdose on something as pedestrian as heroin?" The man went back behind his desk and sat down in his chair. He knew me well. That was exactly what I thought. "But that is not true. I know my son. I know what he is capable of. I know what a complete and total disappointment he is for an heir."

Müller leaned forward, turning his eyes to me, though his body still faced his boss.

"I regularly sweep Junior's bags for drugs," the Swiss supplied, "and our security dogs look for drugs in his belongings all the time. I know what's in his car, I know where he hides his marijuana. Hell, I even know how many condoms he has."

"Well, that's certainly...thorough." I reached out to take up my still unfinished drink. "What can my security company do to help, exactly?"

Rashid sighed once again. I felt complete sympathy for him. He was a billionaire with a level head, an exemplary track record for philanthropy, a corporate culture dedicated to equality, and was cursed to leave his fortune to a complete *eejit*. But that was just bad luck, and the natural way of things, as far as I was concerned. It was tragic, but also predictable. Great things rise, and they inevitably fall. It was the natural cycle of any patrilineal enterprise. Look at every royal family–even the ones whose branches didn't cross like a wreath.

"I think that someone tried to assassinate my son and cover it up to look like a drug overdose," Rashid said.

Müller blinked. That infinitesimal expression from that statue of a man may as well have been a scream of anger. Did he dislike that someone tried to kill his charge under his watch? Was it because it was a near miss? I wanted to crack his head open to see if there was life behind those eyes.

Rashid continued, "I don't know who or why. I have made many enemies."

I couldn't follow the train of conversation. This seemed like paranoia and conjecture. Maybe even the fabrications of a father's mind trying to justify a son's turmoil. The children of successful people often suffered from depression, crippled with the weight of expectations. Maybe that was all this was. An assassination attempt was a giant leap to make.

"If my son does not survive me, then all of my wealth transfers to my cousin," Rashid explained. "He is a wretched man. I suspect he would take my wealth and give it to some... unsavory people. Corrupt people. Do you understand my meaning?"

I understood just fine. The triangle trade. The constant exchange of guns, drugs, and women that fueled the criminal underworld, existing in the ungoverned spaces beneath the veneer of civilization.

"So, give your money to charity if you have no heir." I didn't understand why that wasn't the most obvious solution. "Then there would be no motivation to assassinate Junior at all."

Rashid looked horrified. Then he schooled his features and asked, slowly, "Do you have family, Callum?"

That question hit me in the gut. No, I did not have a family. Not anymore. I had come to my family's wealth too soon, while I was in the service. Any remaining relatives were distant. If an illegitimate child did not come out of the woodwork, then all that I owned would revert to charity or a historical foundation. It was a fate that I had reconciled with a long time ago. All those lush highland mountains and woods, the deer, the fish, the cold winter skies would be owned by people, instead of a person. That seemed right to me.

"None living." I finally answered before the silence grew too heavy.

"Then you may not understand how an act like that would tear my family apart." It was Rashid's turn to look sympathetic. "I cannot do that, you understand?"

My knuckles tightened around the glass. I looked down at golden threads on the enormous red Afghan rug. I didn't have a family to keep together, so I didn't understand.

"So, you want me to help guard Junior on his trip to Argentina." It was a statement now.

"As I have already told Mr. Khan," Müller interjected, his mouth pinched and tense, as though he were trying to keep the words from spilling out of his mouth. "I believe our security is adequate for the trip. It is not necessary for Caledonia Security to get involved."

Was the Swiss statue questioning his boss in front of me? I found that quite amusing and brought my glass to my lips to hide my smile.

"Müller," Rashid chastised, "I simply want assurances and an abundance of caution. This is important to me. Callum, I want you to personally help with securing the boy. Work with Müller and his excellent team."

I took a deep breath. I looked over at the Swiss sitting to my right. He looked back at Rashid who, in turn, looked at his Salvatore Ferragamo oxfords. They were waiting for my response.

I didn't need to keep them waiting long.

I liked the old man. I always had. There aren't too many good billionaires in the world. Surely, I could do this for a person that I considered a friend. He was doing this for family, after all. While I might not have one, I knew the bone-deep pull that they could have, even from the grave.

I stood up. Rashid and Müller followed suit. I reached out a hand and he grasped it with both of his. I felt desperation in its tightness. I smiled at him.

I turned to the sour looking Swiss man and with a clear and determined voice declared, "I look forward to working with you."

CHAPTER THREE

"*Kain na!*" Our mother's shrill cry carried up the stairs, down the hall and to our fragile ear drums. *Eat now!*

"*Oo, Nanay!*" we yelled back in unison. *Yes, mother!*

This was the routine my twin brother and I had fallen into since we were in our thirties and still living with our parents.

When it came time to find a place of our own, we traveled so much that we never did. We were assassins. And on top of that, we were travel nurses. Sure, it was our cover, but we still had licenses to keep up and contracts to accept, so we never settled down enough to try to leave the nest.

We skipped that specific step of life and stayed home, sleeping in our childhood bedrooms.

I sat in my brother's room, legs crossed on the bed. Leo paced back and forth, running a hand through his platinum hair that was growing out to his natural black at the roots.

I glanced through the tinted windows that overlooked the California suburban street. Rows and rows of identical stucco, two-story homes and tiny parcels of green lawns stood against the desert mountains. While each house had a two-car garage, the driveways were all packed with mid-size luxury SUVs and sedans. The garages were just storage spaces in this wasteful middle-class oasis.

Leo's bedroom hadn't changed much since high school. It was plain, with his high school academic ribbons and trophies dominating a wall. I had a similar one in mine, though it was far less distinguished, and much more modest.

"So, you think someone knew that it was you?" Leo said it as if it was the most ridiculous thing in the world.

"Yes. For the last time, yes!" I rolled my eyes in exasperation. "He looked at me, and it was like... he knew."

I couldn't describe how that Scottish guy looked at me. It wasn't with accusation or malice. It was almost in recognition. As if he saw me and *felt* me. Like we had an understanding somehow.

"*Mga Anak!*" the shrill voice called up once again. "*Kain na!*"

My children! Eat now!

If she needed to call us again, she'd be yelling our full government names and might add a Tagalog expletive at the end.

The smell of chicken adobo wafted up the stairs. The soy sauce and vinegar scent filled the house, and I knew my mother was getting ready to set the table. Our stomachs grumbled at the comfort food that awaited us.

Leo stopped his pacing and reached for the doorknob, tugging at his platinum bleached hair. We wore our hair in similar styles. Mine was a little longer, but it was always bleached so we could easily disguise ourselves with temporary hair tint. Quickly changing our appearance was useful, if we need to escape somewhere fast.

I grabbed him by the elbow and brought him in close. Close enough that I could whisper. Close in a way that only twins can be. "We need to talk about a way out."

He pulled out of my grasp. "What are you talking about?"

He didn't like this conversation. I wanted him out of the business. It's not that our line of work was bad–frankly, I kind of enjoyed it. No one ever paid the prices we charged to kill good, innocent people. But Leo wasn't like me. He was the good twin. Like the famous twins of the Gemini constellation, there was always a good twin and... the *other* one. That was me.

The good one is saddled with the burdens that their lesser half heaps onto their giant shoulders and I was growing weary, watching him anchored to my bad decisions. He followed me into this line of work, and now I had to push him out of it.

"Seryoso, kuya," *Seriously, big brother.* I needed him to hear me. I needed him to believe me. "We have enough saved to do what we want. Or we could do nothing! Or... we could *actually* just be nurses. You could even go to medical school."

That would make my parents proud, too. All they knew was that we were nurses, and that's okay with them. But a doctor? Our parents would brag about that to everyone in church until the day they died.

I knew why he didn't use his GI Bill for medical school. It's because I couldn't follow him there. I would never have been able to pass the MCAT. He had a brain for books. I didn't. If he hadn't done my homework, there's a chance I wouldn't have gotten through High School. I learned through hands-on work. If he hadn't been there to push me through nursing school, I probably would have failed out.

He'd never be able to carry me through medical school.

He changed his goals so we could stay together. I think he's regretted that ever since.

"Lea," he growled with irritation. "Just because you think someone noticed you isn't a reason to get out of the business."

He was right. I was using the handsome, red-haired Scotsman as an excuse. He probably didn't notice anything, and even if he suspected me, there was nothing to confirm his suspicions.

"But it might! It's been a good eight years." I knew my voice was getting whiny, but this was how a little sister talked to her older brother, even if he's only older by a minute. "Most people in this line of work either retire or *get* retired like Tito Leo. We're pushing our luck."

Leo's features softened. His brows furrowed. He placed a hand on my shoulder, and I mirrored the gesture.

"Are you scared?" His voice was gentle. Soothing. He wasn't calling me a coward. He just really wanted to understand. I opened my mouth to speak, but was silenced by a banshee scream.

"Leonora Marie and Leonard Marcus Rizal Bonifacio, get down here before I beat you!" our mother yelled in Tagalog.

Outside the house, she sounded like a fully native English speaker. When the shoes came off at the door and she donned those indoor slippers, she transformed into a woman just off the plane from Manila with moving boxes instead of luggage.

We laughed and rolled our eyes and climbed down the worn out, carpeted stairs. It was a four-bedroom, two-bathroom house, with a formal living room and a foyer by the front door for fancy guests. Our mother still kept plastic on that furniture to "keep it nice."

There were never fancy guests. But that didn't stop our mother from treating that space as sacred, just in case the Pope ever came for a visit.

On the big screen TV in the living room, the international news channel played at a low volume. Anchorwoman Calissandra Davenport, in her desert khaki clothes, stood on a windy mountain with a microphone at her chin. She read the number of explosions that had happened around the Baas Medical refugee camps in Kemet.

"Since the discovery of oil under the ungoverned spaces beneath the Kemet Refugee city," she said in that crisp, British voice, "sporadic violence has threatened the humanitarian aid that the area relies on. Business mogul, Alexander Baas, vows to…"

Ligaya Bonifacio, our mother, who we called Nanay, stood at the dinner table, hovering over a large silver pot with freshly steamed white rice. On one side was the chicken stew. On the other was the lumpia, a thin cigar-sized, deep-fried egg roll filled with minced meat. She wielded a giant wooden spoon and pointed it accusingly at us.

"If it wasn't for food, you two would never come out of your rooms!" she said, gesturing for us to set the table. "You spend all your time there and you never clean."

Tatay, the Tagalog title for a father, took his spot at the head of the table. He wore an orange button-down and cargo shorts. His close-cropped hair jutted high on the top, still thick and black despite his age. Since his twin Leopold, or Tito Leo, died five years ago, wrinkles have appeared on the sides of his mouth. His frown lines were becoming permanent.

I smiled at my brother mischievously. "We could always move out, Nanay."

Tatay and Nanay sat at each head of the table. Leo and I took one of the empty seats on either side, caddy-corner to one another. Our table was always ready to seat six just in case we had guests.

Behind Nanay was a huge crucifix with a bleeding Jesus. Behind Tatay's seat was a giant wooden fork and spoon that hung on an empty white wall. That fork and spoon, far too large to serve any purpose other than decoration, had come with their meager belongings when we arrived from the Philippines.

Nanay whacked me on the arm and huffed. "Move out? What for, huh? You don't pay to stay here. Are you too good to live with your parents? I have folded your panties since you were out of diapers." She *tsked* as if it was ridiculous for her thirty-one-year-old adult children to have their own homes. "These ungrateful, spoiled Amerikano kids. They don't appreciate anything."

"I appreciate you," said Leo, coming up from his seat to plant a kiss on Nanay's cheek.

Tatay grunted, which was the signal for everyone to put their palms together for a brief word of grace. Our father's low voice glided over the table, as the smell of the adobo wafted from the hot pan, causing me to salivate.

After we said Amen, the conversation continued as if there was no interruption at all.

I threw a napkin at Leo, who caught mid-air with a chuckle.

"Suck up, much?" I accused.

"I'm the favorite. It's not my fault." He shrugged.

"Anyway," Nanay interrupted, "if you cared about me, you would try to give me grandchildren."

She never corrected him when he claimed to be the favorite. It was simply fact.

"Well, that happened fast." Leo said dryly, raising a brow. "We normally get through the lumpia before you start marrying us off."

"So, I should bring a date back to my mother's house?" I quirked a brow. "That's so romantic."

Nanay reached out with an agile hand and whacked me on the arm again. I suppressed a laugh, and Leo pursed his lips and widened his eyes, wordlessly telling me to be silent.

"Ungrateful child!" she said, shrill and teasing, "I do everything for you and… and… *susmaryosep! Leche!* Why didn't I have more kids? If I had, I would have ten grandchildren already!" She looked up to the heavens as if pleading with the deity to give her strength.

I pretended to massage the arm that she abused and opened my mouth to say something. Leo kicked me under the table, hitting me square below my knee cap. I jumped, my elbow knocking a fork to the floor with a clatter. He mouthed the word "stop" as if he could control how much I teased our mother.

Newsflash. He's not the boss of me.

I leaned down and picked up my fork, wiping it off before putting it back in place.

The doorbell rang. Leo and I threw our heads back and moaned. We already knew who it was. It was the harbinger of mediocrity. The man with delusions of adequacy.

"Children," our father's low voice warned. He glared at us, punctuating his point with a warning finger. "This is my house. We are hospitable to others."

Tatay got up and went to answer the front door. Leo and I smirked at one another, shaking our heads in solidarity when our father's back was turned.

"Hello Leonard!" A distinctly male voice boomed in, sounding like a reality show announcer. "I was just dropping by to see you. I see Lea and Leo are in town."

"Yes, yes." Our father made polite conversation at the door as he invited him in for dinner.

"Of course. He saw our car in the driveway," I grumbled. "He's always spying on us."

"You be nice," Nanay said as she reached over to comb her fingers through my hair. "Brett is a nice boy. Maybe if you two get together, you'll be home more."

"Stop it, Nanay!" I tilted my head away from her hands as she licked her fingers to flatten down a stray frizz. "Gross! And how is he a boy? He must be forty at least."

"This is your fault." Leo crossed his arms and shrugged. "You dropped your fork."

"What does that even mean?"

"No, it's true." Nanay backed him up. Of course she did. "You drop your fork. It means we are having a boy visitor. You drop your spoon, it's a girl."

I couldn't believe that people still recited that bizarre piece of Filipino superstition. I crossed my arms and leaned back in my seat.

"If you spent as much time learning about your heritage," my mother continued, "instead of these Greek Myths, then you would know this already."

"My dropping a fork did not cause him to visit. Leaving our car in the driveway did." What the hell was wrong with my family? "Okay, even if I was going to entertain this old wive's tale, it's possible that the dropping of the fork signaled something that was already going to happen. It could be a warning of a visitor. Not the cause of it.”

Leo shrugged as if he doubted it. He was taking our mother's side because he thought it was funny. *I should have eaten him in the womb.*

“If I drop every spoon in the house,” I continued, “Does that mean an entire sorority is going to come over for dinner?”

Leo grinned. “Try it and see.”

“Ugh, pervert.” I kicked him under the table and missed, stubbing my toe on his chair.

Leo laughed at my expense.

We were going to argue about it more, but a loud voice declared, “You know I love your wife's cooking.”

Leo and I looked at each other, and in one movement, squared our shoulders. To an observant man, the motion would have indicated our double dislike. But our visitor was not an observant man. If he was, he wouldn't have sat right beside me. If he had any awareness, he wouldn't have scooted his chair close and draped an arm across my backrest.

But this was Brett. Brett Bradley. Brett “the douchebag” Bradley.

Brett, who asked for Nanay's permission to take me out, and then wouldn't take no for an answer.

On our first date, he took me to a high-class restaurant. He didn't tip because he got regular coke in his rum and diet. He was sure that the waiter was trying to sabotage his six-pack, as if that was something people did. Brett, who bragged that he had enough money to buy a Tesla S but got a Lexus instead because he didn't want to give in to environmental fascists and their propaganda. Brett, who tried to recruit my father and brother into his bitcoin Ponzi scheme with guarantees of millions in return.

Worst of all, this was Brett. The guy that lived across the street for two months and invited himself to dinner. ALL. THE DAMN. TIME!

Dinner progressed with a new level of politeness, for the sake of our guest.

I pushed my chicken adobo around my plate, completely zoned out from boredom.

"Non-Fungible Tokens!" Brett was trying to explain something to Nanay. When she shrugged, Brett turned to me. "Help me out, Lea. Surely you know what I'm talking about."

Oh shit, this requires my participation. Be a fluffy bunny.

I blinked. Then smiled and shrugged meekly. I had missed the conversation completely. Brett looked at Leo, who mimicked my blank expression.

"Its data stored on a block chain that can be transferred by the owner, and sold and traded for other NFTs." Brett was almost desperate now. "It's the newest form of trading. Like the next level of bitcoin."

Leo and I knew what non-fungible tokens were. Of course, we did. We weren't fucking idiots. We just loved pissing off Brett.

I tolerated him because it stopped our mother from trying to set me up with other worse prospects. Last year, there was a boy from church who wore a pocket protector and tried to tell me they could trace all social justice movements back to Star Trek. The guy before that had a skateboard and an unhealthy Asian fetish. My mother even tried to bring a woman home. She was lovely, but it took her two seconds to realize that I was straight. She was the most acceptable of Nanay's candidates.

No, I dealt with Brett because he was harmless, and better than the alternatives.

Brett pursued me with an off-putting relentlessness that was a source of complete disbelief to Leo. It made no sense. Brett was a good-looking guy. Some would call him very attractive. His personality was odious, but women could overlook that. But, somehow, he was single-minded in his pursuit.

He was Apollo hit with Cupid's arrow, and I was Daphne, impervious to his attention.

My father was so polite that Brett felt comfortable overstaying his welcome. That was Filipino hospitality. It was a politeness our parents tried, and failed, to instill in their American children.

"It's the newest thing, and that's how people make it in today's economy." Brett was still talking. "They have to stay on the cutting edge."

"And that's what you do?" Leo said, his voice pitching low so that it didn't sound like a question, but an accusation. "Stay on the... cutting edge?"

I kicked my brother under the table. When we made eye contact, I widened my eyes to get him to stop. Leo grinned back at me.

"That *is* what I do, Leo," Brett responded, taking it as a compliment. It was very hard, I discovered, not to compliment Brett. "Anyway, enough about me. What about you, babe? How much will I be seeing of you while you're here?"

Brett leaned towards me and smiled, displaying perfect, straight teeth. It was a winning smile, on a great face framed by wavy brown hair, with the soul of a moron too dense to realize that I hated being called *babe*.

"Oh, yes!" Nanay said, clapping her hands with glee. "You two should go out together."

My mouth gaped open. *Et tu, Nanay?*

"I think Leo and I are busy, getting ready for our next trip," I said through clenched teeth. "We don't have a lot of free time between these assignments."

Think of the bunnies. All the fluffy bunnies.

"I'm sure we could find time," Leo supplied, unhelpfully. I kicked him in the kneecap under the table and he winced, but grinned.

I definitely should have eaten him in the womb.

"We'll have to see." I got up without warning and took my plate into the kitchen. "Goodnight, everyone."

This marked that dinner was over. At least for me. What was true for me would also be true for Leo. He followed me up to my room, his hands in his pocket and a teasing smirk on his face.

CHAPTER FOUR

Leo and I sat on my bed cross-legged, facing each other. I was playing with a butterfly knife I often kept in my back pocket. I flipped it open and closed, spinning the slim, flashing blade from one hand to the other. The metal scraped together as it flipped open, before closing with a resolved *click*. The rhythm calmed my heart, slowing down the tension of another interaction with Brett "the Bro" Bradley.

Leo stared at my dancing blade with irritation. "Can you give that a rest?"

I shrugged. "I can, but I won't. It's like a fidget spinner... but sharp."

"Also dangerous."

"We kill people for a living."

"And you want to think about leaving it behind?" Leo said with a sigh. "For what? Brett Bradley?"

I flipped the knife closed; the blade tucked away and struck him on the shoulder while it was in my fist. It thudded loudly against his shoulder.

I would not dignify that with a response.

"We can retire. Kharon can retire," I said as steadily as I could. Kharon was our code name. I had picked it, naming us after the Greek demigod that ferried the souls of the dead over the river Styx. I thought it was fitting. There was always a Greek myth for every occasion. Kharon, more commonly known as the Ferryman, was the entity people hired. Many thought we were one person.

"You can marry Brett Bradley?" he continued to tease. I didn't smile. This was no joking matter.

"Maybe," I said, but there was no conviction in it.

He tilted his head and raised his eyebrow again.

"Okay, not Brett," I agreed, "but maybe I would like to have my own place. To... date. Meet *someone*." I looked at my brother. He continued to look skeptical. "Maybe I could be with someone."

I knew I couldn't. When Leo found someone, then I'd be alone.

I looked over to my desk, where I had a picture of Tito Leo. Beside it was a black candle and rosary. It was my own little memorial for an uncle that I loved like a father.

Leo sighed and stopped smiling. "The Ferryman can't back out of his commitments, but we won't take any more jobs. We have Argentina, then a job in Kemet. That's only a couple of months. We'll talk after that."

"I don't feel good about this Argentina job either." I just couldn't stop. Not now that he promised we could discuss it. I needed to get it all out. "I looked at the target." I looked at the knife in my hands, swinging the blade out and in again. "He had an overdose earlier in the year. Then they ramped up his security and even brought in a second company to follow him around. I don't feel good about that."

"What's the company called?" Leo inquired, quirking a brow.

"How the hell should I know? I didn't look that deep."

When we accepted a job, Leo hacked into emails, accounts, social media... anything that could give us more information on our targets. Enough to understand their pattern of life. If they didn't have any, then we looked at their closest family members and friends. Even the most secretive person had a gabby close friend, secretary, or child that would give away their location, their habits, and tap into their dirty little secrets.

"How is the overdose and the increased security related?" Leo's head tilted to the side. "Talk me through this."

"Because an overdose is the best way to kill him. He fits the profile..." I was pleading for him to understand. "I'm supposed to kill him the same way. Make it look like he partied too hard."

"Okay, talk to me like I haven't been planning this with you so that I can understand what you're thinking." He sat up on the bed and crossed his arms, his brows furrowing into his 'thinking face.' "Communicate with me because I'm not picking up what you're putting down."

"He had an almost fatal overdose while partying in Spain. Then they ramp up his armed security. Sure, it could be because he's going to Argentina, but he's left England before and they didn't give him any additional guards." I looked at Leo for his reaction and found none. "What if that overdose was a failed assassination attempt? Someone trying to copy-cat the Ferryman? This reaction shows that they think it was, no?"

Leo's brow creased, but he said nothing.

I pressed on, "I'd be coming in to do the same thing someone else botched. They're going to be on high alert." He frowned and crossed his arms. "That might be why they brought in more security."

I kept my mouth in a thin line, staring up at him. Bad things are going to happen. I felt it like the sword of Damocles was over my head, held by a flimsy string.

"Sister," he said, his eyes closing in exasperation, "I don't like this business. But you chose this with Tito Leo." He wiped his palm over his face. "You can't just change our course without thinking about it." He tapped my temple. "You and Tito Leo would act before you think. Please, remember, everything you do affects me too. Plan your actions before making choices that will affect us both."

With a high pitched "boop", he tapped me on the nose, then got up and left to go to his room through the adjoining bathroom. He didn't even say goodnight.

Definitely should have strangled him with the umbilical cord when I had the chance.

CHAPTER FIVE

Hot, muggy rain left a romantic sheen on the black sidewalk. The lit store signs reflected on the pavement, giving the whole place an ethereal, urban glow. The target was scheduled to visit the aid camp four hours outside the city. But if we knew anything about our target, he'd shirk his duties and drink his way through the capital instead.

As a precaution, Leo was waiting at the Khan Medical aid camp. It gave Leo a chance to dress wounds and inoculate children. Things he enjoyed doing. On the very unlikely chance that the younger Rashid Khan appeared at the camp, he'd be ready.

That left me stalking the target's favorite brothel. That he *had* a favorite brothel made him a fucking scumbag. He had one in Argentina, Thailand, Germany, and Amsterdam, like a real sex tourist.

He deserves what's coming to him.

I slouched against a red brick wall and pulled my gray hood down over my face. It kept me unremarkable and unseen by the many passing drunken tourists. I even fidgeted with a cigarette to make my prolonged outdoor water excursion a bit more believable.

Three black SUVs pulled up to the curb. As if choreographed, six rear doors opened. Six big men in big suits with small guns tucked into their waistbands came out. They took a few steps, then stood, their hands clasped in front of them, glaring up and down the street, pushing away stumbling drunks who tried to break into their cordon.

Then out came the shaggy-haired target with a punch-able smile on his face. Unlike his sleek entourage, he wore sweatpants and designer flip flops with socks. His t-shirt that probably cost more than some wedding dresses.

He walked toward the one-way glass that marked the front of the brothel. The target clapped his grim-faced security on the back as if they were his old chums. Surrounded by his minions, he went inside, and the SUVs drove away to park in some nearby garage.

After him, four other men stepped out of the vehicles. Unlike the black suits, these guys wore business casual. Black linen pants, steel-toed black shoes, and fitted, un-tucked, button-down shirts. They were around six feet tall. Two were clean shaven, two sported beards.

It was the one with auburn hair that stuck out. I could have picked him out of a line up. My mystery man from the gala. The one who looked at the stars and said he wanted Atalanta.

He walked the way a wolf would prowl, his serious gaze darting up and down the street. He scanned his surroundings, and I averted my gaze before making eye contact. I didn't want him to notice me. Not when he'd inhabited my thoughts for over a month.

In my peripheral vision, I saw him turn to one of his friends. I looked up again to watch him. There was a deep groove between his brows. There was something about his seriousness that made my breath hitch.

Was he the target's friend? God, I hoped not.

He looked at his mates and frowned. One of them rolled their eyes. Another shrugged. Then they walked into the brothel.

I wouldn't be able to follow them, of course.

Places like that had a reception desk. They screened people. This one had exclusive guest lists and required reservations. Just another sign that the target never planned to go to the medical camp.

Instead, I crossed the street. The side of the building was not as glamorous as the front façade of glass and steel would suggest. A thick layer of plaster peeled back, revealing crumbled cement blocks underneath. The elements wore them down, leaving holes just big enough for a couple of fingers to grip into the rough crags.

My burner phone silently vibrated in my pocket. It was a text from an unsaved number. It was our inside man. Per our instructions, he was to inform us of the target's movements, and we would take our orders from him.

Unknown*:* We're in the building.

Tell me something I didn't know, *buddy.*

I climbed the wall using two fingers on each hand. The occasional hole big enough to be used as a toe hold offered me relief until I threw an elbow over the edge of a flat roof deck. There was a metal door that led to a set of stairs. I tried the handle and groaned because it was locked.

Pulling a lock picking kit out of the pouch on my belt, I inserted the metal prods into the small lock. My hand slipped on the rain-wet metal as I held the tension wrench. My other hand tried to push the pins inside. It took three separate tries before I heard the satisfying *click* of the lock opening itself to me.

The phone buzzed again, and I dug it out to see the screen.

Unknown: He's going with the woman now.

I waited a moment.

Unknown: Room 23.

Unknown: Act now!

After a few seconds, another text.

Unknown: Answer me.

I pulled the balaclava over my face, twisted the knob, and let it open. I pulled thin, synthetic gray gloves over my hands. It covered me from head to toe, except for the slits of my eyes.

There was another frantic buzz.

Unknown: RESPOND!

I chuckled, pressed the letter 'K' and clicked send.

I put the phone on silent and slipped it back into my pocket. I made sure the mask was firmly over my face, then stepped down the back stairs.

The balaclava made me sweat. The covering over my mouth and nose kept out the fresh air. Perspiration tickled my nose. It was sour, and hot in my nostrils. The brown hair toner I used for this trip reeked of ammonium. Mixed with my body odor, it was all quite unpleasant.

At the bottom of the stairs was a door that should lead to a hallway. I could hear subdued voices, moans, and rhythmic music. I pushed the door open just a crack so I could peak through. To my left was a red, embroidered curtain with gold tassels grazing the floor beneath, doing very little to block out the cacophony of club music pounding from the distant dance floor. To my right was the hallway.

Small red chandelier lights hung overhead. The walls were covered in red brocade wallpaper, and the floor was painted dark gray cement with red rugs that matched the walls. I followed the room numbers until I found the right one.

Small console tables made of heavy wood stood between some of the doors. Large brass mirrors hung above them. I caught a look at myself in one of them, and it tickled me to see myself in the ninja suit. I looked down at the table. On the surface were stone bowls filled with condoms and travel sized lubricants.

That's some impressive customer service.

CHAPTER SIX

"This Müller is a complete *bawbag*," said George "Geordie" Campbell as we eyed our surroundings with wariness. I had a terrible feeling about this mission. Exactly how terrible everything was didn't really sink in until I found myself in the kind of establishment that I hated the most–a brothel.

It was a high-class one, though. To the untrained eye, it would look like an expensive nightclub. At least until you noticed the clientele. Paunchy, suited men with cigars dangling from their mouths and fingertips were fawned over by scantily clad, beautiful, barely legal women.

Red spotlights danced in time with the thumping house music. Women covered in glitter danced for the male patrons. Occasionally, they'd lead a customer by the hand into adjoining hallways for more *private* interactions.

Müller had a dozen men with him. Six were around the perimeter. The rest were partaking in the wares, sitting at a circular table with Junior.

We arrived at the airport and met Müller's team. But we didn't get into our vehicles to head to the NGO Camp. No, the twenty-something boy in his designer Gucci sandals and overpriced sweatpants arrived a little drunk and made a proclamation.

"Ditch the sad sack camp," the boy said in his British, public-school accent. "I've got a bird to see in town!"

I tried to dismiss my team. Rashid hired us to do security in a medical camp, not entertain some frat boy on his night out. But the boy insisted that we be there. All of us. We normally didn't run missions together. We specialized in different things. We were together to give Rashid his money's worth, with the participation of the industry's best professionals.

I head protection and the preservation of life: personal security, transportation, search and rescue. Geordie was in charge of all our cyber security protocols. I hired Alastair for his eyes. He could hit the wings off a pigeon in San Marcos Square during the height of tourist season. He also had an uncanny ability with a blade. Our Frenchman, Hugo... Well, he was a hammer for which all problems were a nail. Every team needed one of those.

Geordie and I were sitting at the table with Junior, at his insistence. Alastair and Hugo meandered around the perimeter, blending into the cigar smoking crowd and dodging the wanton eyes of women curious about the size of their wallets. I hated places like this. The music thumped too loud, like the throbbing of my pulse during a migraine.

Müller's thumbs were moving quickly on his phone. When he wasn't looking at it, the device sat screen down on the table, his hand laying on top of it waiting for the telltale vibration of a notification. One never seemed to come.

I nursed an untouched drink in front of me. A Macallan. I was committing a mortal sin letting it sit there untasted. Despite Müller's word that this place was secured, none of us believed it. And none of us drank on the job.

Twice, I had tried to insist we go to the camp. Each time, I was rebuffed. I was going to try one more time. A third time was just to clear my conscience and to prove to myself that I had tried.

"Mr. Khan," I raised my voice to be heard over the electronic music. "If we do not go to the Camp, my team and I will report back to your father that our services were not needed, and we'll be on our way."

I was about to stand, but Junior lurched forward to grab my forearm and held me in place. He was built like a bear, not unlike his father. But he didn't observe the same fitness regime that kept that extra midsection from appearing. I could assume that he indulged in rich food and drink and did nothing to work it off.

"No need for that, mate," Junior said, his smile again friendly, and unconcerned. The lack of self-doubt was always a luxury of people in his strata who were too rich to fail. "Why don't you enjoy yourself first? If you must leave, then do it tomorrow."

Müller's phone vibrated. I felt my eyebrows pinch together as the man looked at it and scowled. What had my Swiss friend so agitated? I tilted my head toward Geordie. He was on his own phone, texting away as well. When he sent it, I felt my phone vibrate in my pocket. I didn't pull it out. It wouldn't do for people to notice we were texting each other. Instead, I waited until his phone was gone, and leaned back in my seat.

"I'm on it. We'll offer up Aunt Helen," I heard Alastair say over the radio. Aunt Helen was code for a very specific protocol of ours. We were going to hack Müller's phone.

I watched the plan go into motion with incredible precision. Hugo reached into the inside of his blazer to pull out a small device. He idled to the center of the room, right off the dance floor filled with badly two-stepping men and seductively undulating women. The device blocked all cellular communication. His central location ensured that most patrons would be affected. Then his hands went into his pockets. His part of the plan was initiated.

"*Scheisse!*" Müller said through gritted teeth, clicking at his phone. No doubt, he was turning it on and off airplane mode to jar his reception back to life.

Then Alastair reached into his pocket and turned on his device which triggered anything with wi-fi access to accept terms and conditions that were completely fabricated. It was a standard pop-up that looked like anything the phone may throw up for an update, or for a change of settings. Alastair's device did offer free wi-fi, including internet calling and texting. However, they weren't accepting some free cell service. No. What they were accepting was a Trojan Horse, courtesy of Caledonia Security. It would freeze all the information on that phone in a moment, upload it to our server, and we'd access it later. Every password, every photo, every website would be at our fingertips.

Most of them we'd simply delete and never think about again. I wanted to know what our closed off little Swiss friend was up to. Something about him never quite passed the sniff test.

Müller's eyebrows furrowed. He looked at something on his screen, then frustratingly tapped his phone once...twice...

Then an angry third time with his curled index finger.

He had seen our little pop up. Then his brow relaxed, his lips pursed as his phone came back to life.

Why did a security company have a ready Trojan Horse?

Because when you were protecting someone, the person wanting to cause the most harm was often always in the crowd, quietly stalking, fixated. As creatures for the twenty-first century, our phones are palm sized diaries of our thoughts, our deeds, and everything that bats around in our heads.

"Would you like a drink?" a girl in a sequined, gold mini dress asked. She held a black tray. A white napkin was draped on her forearm.

I gestured to my full glass. She turned her eyes to Geordie who did the same. Alastair and Hugo were at the bar themselves, also nursing full glasses of alcohol, casting clandestine glances around the room.

The girl's friendly smile never wavered.

"Is there anything else you're interested in?" Her voice was raspy, seductive, implying so much more than what was on the bar's menu.

"No, thank you." I smiled at her.

She didn't falter, but simply stood and walked to the next patrons.

I wanted to drink that whiskey.

Buying a woman held no appeal to me, and neither did a woman like Pippa. She thought carnal pleasures were a service she provided in exchange for a ring, a title, and all the marital benefits that came with a high-placed husband.

Nothing but the most enthusiastic, primal consent would ever satisfy me. I'd rather go into the priesthood than be with a woman who treated sex like a chore.

Turning back to Junior, I realized that he was gone. I stood up and scanned the place. I caught a quick glimpse of white sweats with gold lettering as it went behind a curtain that led into a darkened hallway. He would avail himself of someone's services. Where was Müller?

I went to follow the boy. As I was about to tug the curtain aside, a large hand grabbed me.

"No going back there unless you've got a girl with you," growled a burly bouncer, copper skinned with multiple earrings. The tattoo of a cobra twisted around his neck. I needed to get back there, so I looked to my left and my right to ensure that we could not be seen. Other than some glassy, drunken eyes, no one was paying us any attention.

I tugged his arm, pulling the man in behind the curtain and into the hallway. I wrapped an arm around his neck from behind. The rear naked choke. Many people think that chokes are meant to restrict the airflow, but the best techniques restrict blood from traveling to the brain.

The bouncer had been hired for his size, not for his skills.

He kicked, flailed and struggled, trying to rely on his superior height and weight. But he started fading, his limbs growing weak as the blood was kept from his brain.

I gently lowered him to the ground as he lost consciousness.

With the man indisposed, I marched into the red, velvet hall. I wasn't prepared for what I saw. In the subdued lighting stood a hooded figure, his face covered by a gray mask. He was dressed from head-to-toe in gray. He was short, slim with hands balled into fists, knees bent in a combat stance.

Ibiza was an assassination attempt after all.

CHAPTER SEVEN

Lock picking was not my favorite task. Given a choice, I'd rather break in by *breaking* something. Finesse was never my first choice.

The final tumbler clicked. The lock disengaged. I smiled to myself and opened the door after a steady, silent twist.

Showtime. The clock starts now.

The private room was dimly lit, the bed surrounded by velvet maroon brocade. The four-poster bed was of engraved wood.

The room smelled like sex. Not the good kind. Not the kind with the tang of female arousal. It was bad perfume, sweat and hairspray. The woman was on her back, spread wide. A sweaty man was bucking on top of her, grunting like a pig in shit.

Her head popped up and she mumbled something. I didn't understand it.

Ten seconds had elapsed.

It was a dozen steps from the door to the bedside. In those seconds, I confirmed his identity. It was him, alright. Rashid Khan Jr, billionaire boy extraordinaire. The worst-case scenario of nepotism.

Busy with his task, it took a long time for him to realize that death hovered over him.

Then it was too late. I plunged a needle into his bicep and pressed the plunger. He looked in horror as a lump began to form at the injection site. I took the heel of my palm and struck him on the chin, his head cocked back with the slightest of grunts. He fell over in a heap, unconscious. I took that syringe from his arm and threw it across the room. It bounced off a wall then landed on the carpet.

Forty-five seconds.

The woman opened her mouth to scream. I wrapped an arm around her neck from behind and used my free hand as a vice so the blades of my forearm and bicep closed in on the sides of her neck. The pressure constricted the blood vessels on either side of her trachea. It took ten seconds for the restricted blood flow to knock her out. She went limp in my arms and I gently lowered her to the bed.

One minute.

I pulled a blue rubber tourniquet from my bag and wrapped it around her bicep. I found a good vein and took another, smaller syringe of heroin from my med kit and injected it into her blood stream. It might erase the last few minutes of her life from her memory. I was probably doing her a service.

I tossed that needle onto the bedside table.

My eyes went back to Rashid, slumped at the edge of the bed. The lump on his bicep was round, red and would form a bruise. So would the strike on his chin. I took the rubber tourniquet off the woman, then placed it on Rashid's other arm. The third and final syringe was filled with the lethal dose that would kill him. I pierced the needle through his skin, felt the rubbery edges of his vein and injected its contents.

Ninety seconds.

If I got the dosage right – and I always got it right – then it would take a man of his size about 10 minutes to die. His breathing would get shallow. He'd fall into an even deeper sleep, then he'd never open his eyes again.

I put the syringe on the oak nightstand near the lamp with the red, brocade shade.

I grabbed his head on either side and turned him toward the ground, letting him fall off the bed. His chin smacked the edge of the nightstand and he slowly slipped down until his body lay prone on the carpet, his face bent back at a ninety-degree angle, his face against front of the nightstand.

I was here to tell a story.

He tried to inject himself but missed his vein. Frustrated, he threw the syringe across the room. Then it was her turn to partake in this opioid pastime, and she fell asleep under the influence. Then a still frustrated trust fund kid made a second attempt to get high. This time, he got his vein, but in his eagerness, overdosed. He collapsed, hit his chin on the nightstand on his way down – exactly where I had struck him with my palm – and collapsed on the floor, the rubber tourniquet and syringe still in his arm.

Two minutes.

My time was up. He'd be dead in eight minutes or less.

I'll see you in hell, Rashid Khan Jr.

I moved to the open door. The sounds of moans and groans, and screams of theatrically faked pleasure could still be heard in the stillness of the hallway. My eyes scanned the room one final time – and I was satisfied.

I closed the door behind me, ready to leave.

Then I heard it. The scuffle of stifled grunting and the unmistakable sound of flesh hitting flesh.

At the end of the hall, a large man lowered a limp bouncer to the floor. His arm was wrapped around the bouncer's neck.

It was him. The Scotsman from Switzerland. Shit. He couldn't catch me at the scene of the crime for a second time

Fluffy bunnying can't get me out of this one.

"Who are you?" His voice was low, reverberating in his deep barrel chest. But his accent was American. The British voice he used in Montreux was far more convincing. He was faking it.

He stood ready to pounce, hands at his sides, his elbows slightly bent. I could tell by the muscles in his calves and the bulge in his thighs that this guy was...something. I didn't notice it when he was in a tux, but in his work wear, it was obvious that he wasn't just some rich guy or sex tourist.

He wasn't armed. At least not with a gun. In the hallway's red light, his hair was almost crimson. His face was square, made even more angular by the close beard that framed his sharp jawline. A red devil.

He was over six feet tall. Not that it mattered. I was 5'3 in heels. If he was six feet or a million feet tall, it didn't matter. I wouldn't win in a war of punches; his wingspan was too long. He could just put his hand on my forehead, and I'd be swinging at nothing but air.

"Who are you?" he asked again. His voice was gravelly, controlled. I had day-dreamed about it on and off since the gala.

He took a slow step forward. I stepped to the side.

I stood with one foot in front of the other, shoulder width apart. I was wound up, coiled like a serpent waiting to strike. Still, I didn't want to kill this guy. He's not a known associate of Junior. I would know if he was.

I pitched my voice low and over enunciated to sound like a man. He couldn't know that he'd met me before.

"Is that a friend of yours?" I nod to indicate the unconscious bouncer splayed on the ground.

"Listen, buddy, if you walk away now…" he continued. Thankfully, he didn't recognize me, and he did seem to think I was a guy.

His American accent was strong. Too strong. I smirked under my mask, knowing that his deception wouldn't work on me.

He took one more step forward. I took a smaller step back. Tension made me sweat. I felt a cool drop go from my hairline, down the side of my face to my neck.

"Stop moving," I ordered, and he obeyed.

"Okay, friend." He brought his two hands up, palms out as though in a placating gesture. "Who are you here for?"

Things had gone well for the Ferryman. It was just a matter of time before it all fell apart. Things going to shit was just some cosmic rebalancing.

"Who are you?" I turned the question to him.

"I'm just here for a good time." He shrugged. He even tried to smile. It was meant to be a smarmy smile but it looked so unnatural that I let out a disbelieving huff. He was security, no doubt about it.

He looked amazing. As good as when he wore a tux.

I bet he tastes great, too. Something manly, like musk and fresh baked bread.

"Who are you protecting?" I demanded.

I inventoried everything that I had on me that could be used as a weapon. A lock picking kit that could be used as a stabbing implement, but it was small. This guy was enormous. That might be like throwing a dart at a bear. It would just annoy him.

I had a scalpel. It was in my first aid kit. That could work if I was smart with my cuts.

He was starting to circle, and I moved to counter. Constrained by the small space, we were just inches out of arm's reach.

"Just some rich, harmless kid, pal. No one important." His fake American accent bothered me. I wanted to hear his real voice. The one I'd heard in the moments when my mind idled.

"The younger Rashid Khan," I enunciated his name perfectly. It was breaking my heart that he was the extra security that had been hired for my target. I don't know why it bothered me so much that he was the one standing opposite me. "Human trafficker and trust fund kid who has been to this particular brothel no less than half a dozen times in the same number of years."

He had the decency to look shocked. That was different. Maybe he really didn't know who he was working for.

"No." His voice has taken on a slight waiver, almost as if he was convincing himself. "That's not true." His tone had an upward inflection. It was a question.

"You don't know anything about the person you're protecting, do you?" My fingers twitched, and my posture relaxed.

Poor guy has no clue, does he?

He'd still kill me, though, and I would kill him if I had to. I tried to slowly, unnoticeably, get my finger to the med kit on my hip.

"Maybe not," he said, "but if that's true, then there are other ways to handle it other than an extrajudicial killing."

"Other ways?" I mocked. There were no other ways. Courts? The intervention of his father? Public pressure? None of that would work.

I slowly unzipped the medical kit. I just needed a small opening. Just enough to get that cold, slim handle out with my left hand.

"I can promise you that I can fix this." He seemed earnest, his shoulders losing some tension as he seemed to be thinking about my words. "I can make sure he sees justice."

"And who are you?"

"I'm Callum MacLachlan, and my word is my bond." He said it as though that name should mean a damn thing to me. He held out his hand for a handshake. "And who are you?"

It was strange to finally have a name to associate with that face.

My fingers reached for the scalpel, staring at his outstretched hand. Despite his cajoling, and that honest *awe shucks* look in his eyes, he wouldn't hesitate to knock me on my ass.

I smirked.

I leaned forward and reached out one gloved hand, my other still touched the scalpel's handle. Our palms met, and fingers clasped. His hand was warm, large, and strong. Huge hands, huge man... huge...

He pulled me into him, taking me off balance, but I anticipated this. Short people, more so than our vertically blessed counterparts, understand that gravity is our friend. I followed the momentum and squatted low to the ground. I planted my feet and drove my shoulder into his hip hinge. He toppled forward and over my back.

He smelled like the forest. Like grass, and earth, and a cool breeze. I got a hint of his skin, his musk, his scent. No. He didn't smell like the forest. He smelled like how it would feel to make love in a forest.

With half his weight spread above me, I used his instability against him. I hooked my right arm behind his knee and brought it to my chest. Standing, I pulled his leg out from under him. He fell back hard, his head cracked on the floor. I brought up the scalpel with my left hand and the metal glinted in the sparse light. I arced it down to his neck.

His thick forearm glanced it away from his face. It embedded into the space between his neck and shoulder, a few inches from his external carotid. He bled fast, but not as fast as if I had cut his artery. Still, the red pool spread beneath him on the black cement.

He didn't sputter or moan. His eyes closed and his breaths slowed as though he was just going into a deep, anesthetic sleep.

This is what the action movies get wrong. They require huge blows, tons of blood and explosions to kill someone. But mammals are fragile things. It only takes a little more than a pound of force to break human skin. Even less to get through all the fatty, muscly bits. It's amazing how any of us ever survive.

His light was flickering away, his eyes closed and lolled to one side.

I crouched over him, careful not to step in the blood, and placed a hand near his face. I didn't feel any hot air to indicate that he was breathing. Then again, that could have just been my glove getting in the way. I touched his neck. There was still a pulse.

I should pull the scalpel from his neck and let him bleed.

The job was fucked. No one would believe that Junior overdosed, not with this downed bodyguard in the hallway. There was only one question I needed to answer: Is it better for the witness to be dead or alive?

It would be so easy just to pull out the scalpel, opening the wound and the blood. He'd bleed out in seconds. That was the safer choice for me.

But I didn't want this guy's light to be extinguished. At least not by my hand. He didn't deserve that.

In his ear was a small device. It was white. Like the Bluetooth earphones that were popular nowadays. But it was different. It had more buttons and was a little bigger. I pulled out the radio from the conch of his ear. It was perfectly shaped to his ear canal, a customized radio. I could hear a faint voice coming from the little speaker. Someone was talking on the other end.

"Callum, do you read me?" the voice was faint, with a Gaelic accent. Maybe another Scotsman?

Leo and I thought about creating a similar earpiece in case he and I had to work together. But the reason to get them never happened.

There was a clicker on the outside, operated by touch. I started touching it, and I heard the beep through the tiny speaker. I gave it three short touches, three long ones, then three short ones again. I did this sequence three times before dropping it into the pool of blood.

He only had a few minutes to live. Maybe someone would save him.

CHAPTER EIGHT

The darkness was thick. I reached out my hand, grasping for something—anything. A gray, gloved hand reached back. I was tumbling through the air, falling face down. The blackness turned red, and my body felt heavy. Rigid.

I was dying. Quietly and alone. Leaving nothing behind.

Beep. Beep. Beep.

I hated that fucking smell. It was the smell of antiseptic, pine-scented industrial cleaning products, cranked up air conditioning and Geordie's burned coffee. I could always smell it. It was this weird, French press that was more beans than water. Bitter, dark, and could peel paint.

I was in a hospital. I knew that before opening my eyes. I could hear the rhythmic whirl and clicks of machines. That endless, steady low beeping was impossible to ignore.

My eyes were heavy, my lashes pasted together by sleep, sweat, and tears. I was in a bed, wired up to IVs. My shoulder felt like it was fresh from a meat grinder. Everything in this room was white. The walls, the tile floors, the ceiling and even the air-pressured doors. The very picture of modern sterility.

Geordie sat to my left, on a chair pulled next to a wall. He furrowed his brow as he stared into a Styrofoam cup. He sat, frowning in a wee, mass-produced chair, looking pathetically forlorn.

"What's with that sour puss?" I croaked out. My voice rubbed at my throat like sandpaper. *Fuck. What happened to me?*

"Jesus!" Geordie jumped. "I thought we might lose you. Do you know how much blood we had to pump back into ye, man? The Duchess of Bathory would have thought it was too much."

"I'm too tired for obscure references." I couldn't help a little smirk.

Everything hurt. I wiggled my toes and flexed my ankles. I worked my way up and bent my knee, just a little, one by one just to know that they still worked. My arms still felt like they functioned. But that left shoulder... There was a searing pain that went from the shoulder to the little tendons on my neck. But that was nothing compared to the overall exhaustion that I felt in every cell of my body.

Then it all started coming back to me. The night. The wee man. I could still feel him lunging, that sharp shoulder burying into the hinge of my hip as I fell to the ground. He took my legs out from under me. It was like being outmaneuvered by a whip.

"Did you see who it was?" Geordie's voice gentled.

"Skinny, short. He must be less than 11 stones... covered from head to foot in gray." I gave the physical description that I could remember. "The eyes were brown. Very dark, almost black. Tan, from what I could see of their skin."

Even the hands were small, but strong. The kind that swung an ax.

"All the doors were closed when it happened," I reasoned. "I think they know how to pick locks."

"Aye, the door was unlocked. The woman said that it was locked from the inside when they got started."

"The woman?" He gave me a chagrined look. He meant the working girl Junior had been with. She was alive then. "Is Junior...?"

I let the question hang in the air.

Geordie shook his head, slowly, gravely. "Overdosed. The girl had heroin in her system as well. She remembers nothing. She woke up on the bed with him dead on the floor."

"Poor girl." And poor Rashid. The mission failed. Everything had gone completely sideways. Fuck!

"Mr. Khan is devastated, of course. He wanted me to extend his thanks to you." Geordie sounded exhausted. "I found you bleeding out in the hallway, a scalpel in your shoulder. Do you remember signaling me?"

"No." I tried to wrack my brain. I didn't have the wherewithal to signal for him.

It wasn't my first failed mission. But it was the first time I had ever lost a client.

"I heard it on the radio." Geordie tapped his earlobe to indicate our earpieces, then scooted his chair closer to me. "I cannae believe that I recognized it. Morse code. You did it three times using the squelch. The old SOS."

"Morse code? Who the fuck uses morse code? I haven't done that since... Kosovo?" I felt my brows pinch together, then looked at Geordie who seemed equally confused as he frowned before sipping his coffee.

"I was surprised too, that's why I came so fast." Geordie was sitting up straighter and throwing his free hand up in a perplexed gesture. "I called help fer ye first. I didn't even check on Junior. I didna think anything was amiss until I heard the wee lass scream behind the door. It was too late."

Remorse. That's what was in his eyes. I caught the faint smell of cigarettes on his breath. He'd quit for years. It'd be terrible if I was the reason he would relapse.

"Can you remember anything else about the man who did this?" he continued.

I thought back.

I couldn't remember much. He spoke English with an American accent, but that meant nothing nowadays. Even I could speak American if pressed. It was standard for people in our line of work, as they are the most populous native English speakers.

"They smelled... tropical. I don't know," I admitted. "I don't know. It was faint."

"The laddie smelled fine, then?" Geordie's eyebrow arched and he smiled. "Did ye get a little intimate? Did ye like it?"

"Fuck you, *eejit*." I wanted to holler at him, but only managed a croak.

It wasn't funny, but I knew he was grasping at anything to lighten the mood. He reached up his free arm and stretched. I heard his back crack. I wondered how long he'd taken up residence in that chair. His hair was mussed, he had bags under his eyes and deep grooves wrinkled his shirt where the arm rest cut into his side.

I tried to swallow, but my mouth was dry. I coughed instead.

"It's no' my fault you had your arse skelped by a wean." He meant a child. "I'm sorry, but here's what I know from you. This dwarf of a villain was dressed like a gray ninja, picking a lock. He took you down in hand-to-hand combat and the weapon they used to hurt you was a Baas Medical scalpel. Oh, and they smelled like a sweet tropical flower. Is that the long and short of it?"

It was improbable when it was happening. Yet, there it was.

"Baas Medical, you say?" I centered in on those words. "You found something on the scalpel?"

"They left it in your neck, so it was covered in your blood." He winced. It must have been a lot of blood if it made his stomach turn. "Good thing, too. They said if the wean had pulled it out, you might have bled out. I cleaned it off and I tracked the serial number."

"There are serial numbers on scalpels? Like...on guns?" I asked.

"I'd never heard of it either." His eyebrows rose as he shrugged. "Your buddy Baas puts them on there. He's a bit of a control freak, isn't he? He just likes to be able to know if someone's using his equipment." Geordie shrugged as if that was a totally normal thing to do.

The door opened and closed. My eyes were unfocused, and it took a moment for them to decipher the newcomer's face. Müller. That Swiss bastard. I looked over to Geordie who shrugged.

"Callum," Müller greeted.

Feeling sour, I grumbled, "Please, call me MacLachlan. Only my friends call me Callum."

Geordie tried to hide his smile behind his cup.

The expressionless Swiss just continued to stand there, looking at me. The silence hung heavy. Several things went through my mind at once. First was that I'm in this because of him. His inadequate security, the fact that he enabled his charge to change plans at the last minute, and never communicated were just some of the reasons things went tit's up. He was the reason why Rashid Khan's enormous wealth was very likely to go to his cousin, who would use it to fund the Kemet National Front, or KNF.

He was the reason why Rashid Khan's son was now dead.

It wasn't even anger or rage that went through me. A feeling started down in my gut and rose towards my chest. It was contempt. Scorn. Disgust. He was a disgrace to our occupation.

"As I was saying," Geordie grunted, his lips curling in disgust as he turned away from Müller, "I found some information on the scalpel's serial number..."

"We'll talk about it later," I interrupted him.

I didn't know why, but I wasn't going to allow Müller to hear about the little ninja. I would never work with him again. It bothered me that the unblinking psychopath was standing over my bed. What the hell was he doing here?

"MacLachlan," Müller's voice was giving me a damn headache. "I'm here on behalf of Mr. Rashid who hopes you recover from injuries soon and hopes that you intend to find the person or people responsible for the loss of his son."

"Aye," I said, "But we shan't do anything until our team is operational."

"I understand," Müller nodded, grimly.

"Do you?" I don't try to keep the venom from my voice. "Because you said that place was secure. That entire thing was shite from the get-go and I ended up getting stabbed in the neck trying to save the mission."

Hospital bed be damned. I was not going to have this man standing over me and bear none of the responsibility for what happened. I tensed, trying to sit up, but the weakness kept me from raising anything but my head.

"I know we have had...differences," Müller said with a completely straight face. I was impressed by the delivery. "But it would be best if we work together on this now, to bring closure for Mr. Rashid."

"We'll be doing our own investigation," Geordie said aggressively, reading my intent and backing me up like a true brother.

"I'm sure you'll understand why," I sneered at Müller before he could try to counter.

Müller's pale eyes darted back and forth between the two of us before he nodded and left. We waited a few minutes before Geordie jumped from his chair, opened the door, and looked up and down the hallway, just to be sure that he was gone.

"I really don't like that prick," Geordie said, slumping back into the chair. "Hugo and Alastair are fine by the way. They stayed a few days waiting for you to wake up, but then went to New York City. Something about tickets to an underground fight. I'll let them know you're alive, though."

I looked up at the ceiling, trying to relax. I took in a deep breath, registering the sights, sounds and feelings to ground me in the present moment. The smell of his coffee, the white, square lights overhead, the feel of the plastic covered bedding underneath me. "How long was I out?"

"Four days now," Geordie said. "When you're stable, we'll get you back to Scotland."

"Sounds lovely."

The mission was a failure.

Junior was dead. Rashid was, rightfully, devastated. This can't be salvaged. Maybe we could find the assassin and bring them to justice, but that wouldn't bring Rashid's son back to life.

I brought a hand up to my face, at the irritated skin there.

I closed my eyes and tried to breathe deeply. Slow inhales, slow exhales. Count to four at every breath. Try to breathe the pain away.

Rashid's son was gone. The poor old man had lost his only boy, his life would be turned upside down, when he had trusted me to be there for him. My eyes were starting to sting as a deep pit in my chest opened up.

Rashid would be well within his rights to cut ties with me at this point. He was giving me a chance to try to make amends, and that was as much a testament to his graciousness than anything else.

Geordie coughed beside me. He waited for me to look at him. With considerable effort, I let my head fall to the side so I could see him sitting in the chair. Geordie had a tablet out. It was a bit of a monstrosity, padded with black rubber to make it crash proof and waterproof. It could even withstand an explosion or two.

"While you've been napping," he deadpans, "I was doing some research. I found out who bought the scalpel. I called in a favor from our friend, Alex." Geordie and I had gone to the same school. He and Alex were classmates too. But Geordie never called him a friend. "He was very helpful after I told him it was for you. By the way, since you're alive, you now owe him a favor. I assume it'll be something sexual, but I told him you'd be good for it..."

"For fuck's sake, I'm wounded, and already with your cheek." I rolled my eyes, slamming my head back onto the pillow.

"As I was saying," he interrupted, punctuating his words with the lift of a single finger to shush me, "The scalpel led back to a TABI PO Medical Company. They have this PO BOX near Barstow, California. It's really a small-time operation with a couple of nurses who take contracts in understaffed ICUs."

He stopped speaking, then typed on the screen with his thick finger.

"Are ye going to tell me more, or was that all you got?" I prompt. He didn't respond but kept typing away. "Or are you doing this to keep me in suspense?"

He took his eyes off the screen just long enough to give me a dirty look.

"The company only has two employees. Siblings, in fact." He spun the tablet in his hand so that the screen was facing me. "Does this guy look familiar?"

I looked at the ID photo of an olive-skinned man. He had thick lips, a flat nose and thick, bleached platinum, almost white, hair that was long on top, and came down the sides of his broad forehead in curtain bangs. Geordie swiped to the next photo. It was an image of the same guy, but he was shirtless at the beach. His muscles were wiry, the shoulders defined. His pecs perfectly square, and he had an enviable eight pack. I could see every striation on his lean form.

I'd never have an eight pack. Highland stock threw around tree trunks for sport. We weren't built to be wiry like that. We had to withstand harsh winters. This man belonged on the beaches. I bet he lived on fruit and coconut water.

Geordie moved on to the next image. It was of him on the edge of a cliff, two fingers of each hand holding on to an overhang while his legs dangled precariously beneath him. He was laughing. The muscles of his back showed every sinew. The guy might have a slight build, but there was genuine power there.

"I think that could be him, but I don't know." I wished I could shrug, but all I could manage was a grimaced approximation of it. "Like I said, I could only see his eyes. The build looks right, though. He was strong as fuck."

Geordie turned the screen back towards himself. "That's Leonard Bonifacio III. He's a travel nurse. The other employee under that Tabi Po company is his twin sister. I'm not sure if you're even going to believe what I've found about the two of them. It's really just..." He let out a disbelieving sigh. "A'right, so... Leonard and his sister, Leonora, are both nurses..."

He said that the twins were 31, born in the Philippines but living in Los Angeles. He joined the navy out of high school and became a corpsman. She joined the Army and became a medic.

"That's the longest separation those two have ever had. As soon as they were done with their commitments, the two went back to LA and completed their Bachelor of Science in Nursing." Geordie was typing as he spoke. "They completed the program together, then established that medical company. They've been contracting themselves out ever since." Geordie looked up, flipped the screen back towards me so that he could show me a map. "I looked at every place he has traveled in the past 4 years and in almost every location, there has been a death. No murders, no assassinations, no investigations. Just suicides or accidents. It took a while, but I looked into Medical Board rosters to see which companies hired Tabi Po, and look at this."

He stood and brought the screen in front of my face. There was a spreadsheet with several deaths and the general location of each sibling.

Three months prior, a human trafficker was found dead in Thailand. It was an internal conflict. Leonard was in-country, inoculating rural children with a Catholic Charity about an hour away. The list of coincidences went on and on.

Last month, Ivan Leclerc accidentally drowned in Montreux, Switzerland. I remember that one. I fished him out. Both he and his sister were there on Bass Medical's payroll to attend the Gala.

"Wait," my eyes narrowed as I looked at his face. There was a thought niggling in the back of my head. He bore a resemblance to someone. "Show me the sister."

Geordie clicked around and turned the tablet to me.

It was her. Atalanta, with her faddish hair, chocolate brown irises and those cold eyes that could pierce through a man like a bullet as she verbally tore him apart. My own beautiful woman who slipped from my fingers when Ivan interrupted the proceedings with his untimely death.

I needed to protect her, from the consequences of her brother's actions, so I kept silent. Because the alternative was that she was... *No. That couldn't be.*

"And that's not the most disturbing part." Geordie turned the screen and clicked around again.

"What could be more disturbing than a nurse murdering people?" This was not the profile I was expecting. I was expecting a little ninja with a lot of backing. Maybe a high-tech lair and a reputation for brutality and ruthlessness. Maybe a KNF hitman or something of that nature.

"Well, it's their personal life." Geordie looked like he couldn't quite believe what he was about to say. "They live with their parents. The two of them share a single car. I cannae find a whole lot of spending and no debts. Their biggest purchase was paying their parent's mortgage. I just can't…wrap my head around the fact that this *Leonard* is the killer. Ach, it's even in the *name*… What assassin is called Leonard?"

I chuckled. It was not a superhero name, by far. But a name is just a name. A viper by any other name would still be as deadly.

"Let me see that picture again." I weakly reached with a hand.

Geordie handed me the tablet with Leonard's face on it. Black eyes stared back at me. The eyes are deep, intelligent and wide, slightly almond shaped. Those were the eyes I looked at in Argentina, but it didn't feel quite right. "He certainly looks right."

I didn't dare consider that my Atalanta could be a murderer. With that easy laugh, and smile? No way.

"A'right," Geordie acknowledged. "So, I did some digging. I found some people taking credit for hiring for some of those hits. Apparently, online, he goes by the name Kharon and will only do jobs for people who pay their fee up front, and they must be referred."

"What's a Kharon?" Some of these self-determined code names could give insight into their mentality.

"It's from Greek Mythology. The guy that takes you over the river Styx to Hades. He's more informally called the Ferryman."

I hadn't taken my eyes off the guy's photo yet. I'd need to see him in person to be sure if it was him or not. I'd need to catch that feeling, or scent.

"So why didn't the Ferryman take me across the river?" I pondered. Someone tapped morse code into my headset to save me. Was that him? "Why did he call for help instead of just ending me?"

Geordie looked at me. He blinked. Then he shrugged. "I don't know. Maybe he's just a nice guy who smells braw and kills people?"

"Can a highly sought-after hitman be a 31-year-old male nurse who still lives with his mum and doesn't even have his own car?" As far as I was concerned, this was the real question of the day.

"If I lived with my parents, I'd be driven to murder." Geordie smiled. "Are you ruling her out?"

"I just don't think it's her." I shrugged. I wasn't sure if I believed it. "I spoke to her. She was kind, and funny. I just don't... think it's her."

I didn't want it to be her. I wasn't ready to confront why I felt that way, but the urge to defend her was strong.

"Aye, it's a well-known fact that assassins cannae have a sense of humor." Geordie's sarcasm was as thick as his coffee today.

"What about financials?" I changed the subject. "There must be traceable money."

"Aye, he has money. So does she. But that can all be explained away by the travel nursing and extensive solar farming—"

"What the hell is solar farming?" I interrupted, my head popping up again, before the pain made me drop back onto the bed.

"It's incredibly lucrative, or so I've discovered. It's solar panels. They have acres of them, and they sell the power back to electric companies." Geordie mirrored my surprise. "The travel nursing is quite a boondoggle, too. They make more than some doctors. If the two of them wanted, they could buy neighboring houses in Beverly Hills and drive Aston Martins."

"What kind of car do they drive?"

"A fifteen-year-old Audi A3."

"None of this makes any sense."

"I don't think he wanted to kill ye. They only wanted Junior, and that's what he did."

"They're intentional about their kills."

"That's what I've traced so far. There's never collateral damage. There's never a bodyguard or family member in the room that gets taken out. No accidental killing of a janitor or doorman. They're either extremely lucky, or extremely purposeful." Geordie almost sounded impressed. "That's why he's so expensive. He makes no mistakes."

I pondered that. A perfect assassin. What could I deduce from that information alone?

"Well," Geordie said with a little grin on his face. "No mistakes until you. I assume we'll be getting some good old-fashioned revenge when you're back in shape."

I let out a long exhale. "Thank you for finding me, Geordie."

"Shut your gob." He sounded annoyed. "You know, chocolate is thicker than whatever it is…"

My mind went back to our days at St. Michael's. It was a short childish poem that had been recited in the dormitories year after year. Usually, it was whispered in the dead of night, when the loneliness of being a geographical orphaned overwhelmed the frail, young heart:

Out of sight, out of mind in alpine mud,

You learn fast that chocolate is thicker than blood.

It wasn't profound, or even witty, but it stuck in our juvenile minds, and we wore it like armor. It bonded us closer than family. It was what connected me to Geordie, to Alex, to a network of "chocolatiers" all over the world. When we had no families, we had each other.

What more could we ask for in this world?

CHAPTER NINE

The Ferryman's lair was an enormous piece of property in the Mojave Desert owned by our umbrella company, Tabi Po LLC. We named the company as a joke. "Tabi, Tabi Po" was a phrase used to ask for the forgiveness of ghosts, goblins and dwendes when entering a haunted area. It was a way to beg mischievous spirits to let you on your way when going through spiritual territory.

I didn't fall for Filipino folklore like Leo did. He thought it would help us get the favor of malevolent spirits when doing heinous work like this. The good run we had, to him, was proof that Filipino deities still wielded power in this world.

We needed a place far from home to do our assassin-type things and settled on this piece of land.

The land cost almost nothing. It was so thoroughly dead that it boasted nothing but cliffs, hard, dry dirt, rocks and a Cold War missile bunker. Its regular inhabitants included some endangered turtles, as well as the occasional mangy looking donkey.

The bunker was accessed by a hatch peeking over the ground, about the size of a manhole. It was a rusted-out thing with a wheel on top to open it. A narrow ladder led down into a large, empty room with a cylindrical roof. The walls were rusted, the desert beige paint was peeling.

Nothing grew on this large piece of dirt. There might be some desert brush, but there could be nothing agricultural.

We put up some solar panels. If anyone asked why we invested in this space, we said it was because we were solar farmers, harvesting energy. We owned and operated acres upon acres of solar panels around the desert. While we were gone, we hired local maintenance men to do regular checkups. The power we sent back to the grid generated a small income. We siphoned a small amount to our bunker to power the air conditioner and the various computers and satellites we used to connect to the grid.

The profits amounted to a small fortune we sent to an offshore bank account.

Still, the bunker looked like a piece of shit.

If it didn't require repairs because the structure was crumbling, we didn't bother to fix it. These rusted walls stayed rusty, the coyote-colored paint stayed cracked. The air conditioner and the bunker's position underground kept it cool. The only new things inside were the servers that we ran, and the multiple screens that covered the main wall. On the other side, we built a few small rooms from plywood. Those were our rooms in case Leo and I decide to sleep here. Between us was a shared bathroom.

Our bedrooms were mirror images, just like in our parent's home.

We always said that we'd improve it, but we didn't. What we had was good enough. It'd be silly to wish for more.

I sat in front of the computer monitors. One of them had the CCTV footage of the large funeral in the United Arab Emirates. In a large, ornate mosque, there was a funeral procession for the son of a billionaire. The son that I killed. Mourners wailed loudly as the body, wrapped in a white shroud, was laid to rest.

I ran my fingers through my hair. The brown toner was fading out in favor of the platinum bleach underneath.

I caused the grief on the television, but I didn't feel bad about it. Leo always told me it would be okay if I felt bad. That it was *normal* to feel bad. Or at least to feel *something*. But there was nothing there.

"Well-known philanthropist and businessman Rashid Khan grieves for the loss of his son today." Callisandra Davenport's voice narrated as the camera panned over a grieving crowd. "The younger Khan was found dead in his hotel room while on a humanitarian mission to underserved communities in Argentina. There are rumors of foul play."

Twirling the butterfly knife in my hand, I looked through the printout of Rashid Junior's Swiss bank accounts. They would have been un-hackable had it not been for Junior's overall stupidity. He used his own birthday for pins, and passwords all used variations of his favorite word — pussy.

I hated to be so cynical about mankind, but I was right so often that it was simply fact. Most men are stupid creatures.

The money coming into his account was from the sick triangle trade. Drugs from South America and Central Asia were sold in the streets of Europe and the United States. The profits were then used to buy guns which are sold to the many conflicts around the world. The revenue from that were then sent to Eastern Europe, South America and Asia to buy humans. They were trafficked for more profits, which then bought drugs, then guns...then the sick, sad cycle went round again.

Rashid Junior operated at two points of the triangle. He profited from humans and drugs. That was his domain and his responsibility. Arguably, it was the most disturbing apex. I was less critical of the weapons, since they were only as bad as the people who wielded them.

I was running a search for the name Callum MacLachlan. There was no death announcement. He wasn't checked into a morgue in Argentina, and there's no record of him being taken to an emergency room. I even went so far as to look for any white foreigner that matched his description getting checked into the hospital at around the time everything happened. There was nothing. It was like he wasn't even there. I didn't know if he was dead or alive.

I frantically looked for any scrap of information on him.

What started as professional curiosity soon turned into rabid fascination.

His full name? Callum Euan Edmund MacLachlan of MacLachlan, Chief of Clan MacLachlan, 27th of MacLachlan and Baron of Strathlachlan... That was one hell of a mouthful.

He was the only child of some other guy who was the 26th of Maclachlan. His father died of lung cancer. His mother passed a year later as a result of a fatal car accident. He was in the SAS at the time and had to be pulled out of his deployment to Kandahar.

He owned two castles in a place called Argyll and Bute. One was old and historic. It was a ruin. The other castle was new, with full amenities and could be rented out to wedding parties and receptions. You could even buy a night's stay there.

It was pretty swanky.

He was also a well renowned philanthropist. He spent lavishly at galas and charity balls, looking dapper in evening tuxedos. Supermodel, Lady Pippa Fox, was often on his arm. They were often in matching colors. He'd wear a dapper red tie or pocket square, and she'd be in a long, scarlet gown that left nothing of her perfect body to the imagination. Despite their supposedly broken engagement, which wasn't in any of the papers, they still seemed quite courteous to each other. Maybe they weren't broken at all. Maybe they were together still.

Maybe he was lying to me. Men lie to women they're not related to. I was probably putting too much affinity on a conversation that lasted only minutes.

Surely, Baron MacLachlan, or whatever the right title was, would have a funeral fit for a Lord? If he was dead, there'd be a ceremony or announcement.

People with castles didn't just die without fanfare.

I stared at the pictures of him, and the numerous data points that made up his life. His resumé was perfectly fine, full of accolades, awards for valor and the usual congratulatory bullshit common among officers. But it was his personal financial statements that I found perplexing. He started his own private security company, hiring veterans coming out of the Global War on Terror. Then he donated to several charities. There were endowments to help sick children get long term care at home, instead of at the hospital. A charity that did the same for geriatric patients. There were scholarships and schools... The list was never ending.

I stared at his pictures and the way he smiled. His green eyes always sparkled like there was some joke that only he was hearing.

I vividly remembered his hand in mine. His large, veiny hand felt calloused. My hands were calloused as well, but shit. His were something else. This was a man who probably lived on protein shakes, creatine and heavy lifting. It would have been intimidating for a normal person to go up against him.

I had taken him down, but that didn't detract from his visceral, primal nature. In the olden days, he would have been a knight, or a Viking, banging tavern wenches and rescuing damsels.

He was the kind of guy that could make me feel... delicate.

I hope he's alive.

CHAPTER TEN

I WAS BACK, STARING out the floor to ceiling windows of Rashid's office overlooking the Thames. Rashid wore an all-black suit. White flowers covered the floor and desk, each one proclaiming sympathies for the loss of an only son.

Rashid's hands shook as he held his whiskey glass, the ice clinking against the sides. He had bags under his eyes, and his temples were starting to gray. He slumped in the chair behind his desk, looking defeated.

My fingers tapped on the armrest of my seat; my body vibrated with so many unanswered questions.

Geordie flew ahead to Scotland to go through everything we pulled from Müller's phone.

The assassin's voice was still in my head – *You don't even know who you're protecting, do you?*

Bank statements could confirm the assassin's accusations. Unfortunately, we couldn't do any forensic accounting on Junior's Swiss bank accounts. Those banks were an impenetrable wall. It didn't matter if you represented the family of the recently slain, the victim of a global tragedy or the survivor of systemic genocide. The Swiss bank only cared about one thing: correct documentation.

To the Swiss, bureaucracy was the highest form of morality.

Maybe Rashid Senior had some documentation for his son's bank accounts, but I could hardly ask him for access. How would I explain that? *Sorry your son's dead, but can I access his accounts to find out if he's a human trafficker?*

"I have gotten your report." Rashid turned his head towards me. He placed his hand on a blue folder. The silver Caledonia Securities logo - a stylized compass, abstract rose and twin Scottish lions - was stamped on the front. "Müller, for his part, took responsibility for his own failings."

That surprised me. I expected to go head-to-head with the man. I thought it would be his word against mine. I refrained from asking what Müller's side of the story had been.

"Do you know who did it?" Rashid's eyes were lined with red as he stared at me. "Müller has found no trace of the killer. We have looked at everyone in the club, looked at every camera going in and out. We have interviewed everyone that was there, and they know nothing! Did you see who did it?"

He was loudly breathing through his nose. His fists were shaking with barely controlled rage.

"I saw him before he stabbed me. But his face was covered."

"Müller says there are rumors that it is the work of someone called the Ferryman. That he's some boogeyman that kills without leaving any evidence." His voice choked before he continued. "He mentioned that it was on some...dark web or whatever that means. They make it look like an accident. Do you know anything about this?"

Yes I do. "No, I haven't heard anything yet."

Lie. Lie. Lie! I was lying to a friend, and for what? To find out why the Ferryman hadn't finished the job on me? To find out if the word of a murderer was worth trusting? *Fuck!*

Rashid somberly nodded. His entire body reeked of defeat.

For a moment, we both stared out into space. Him, probably to bask in his grief. Me, to bask in my failure.

These things deserved to be felt. And felt deeply.

"Would you like another drink?" Rashid jumped up and went over to his glass bar.

"No," I indicated my still full glass.

He pulled out the Macallan and poured himself a healthy glass. He damn near filled the entire tumbler then drank it in one swallow.

"I want him." His voice was thick and determined.

"Who?" I was playing dumb.

"Whoever killed my boy," he snapped.

I took a breath, trying to center myself to not be pulled by his emotions. "I can understand that."

"I don't think you can." Rashid's eyes came off his glass and he looked at me. Straight at me with piercing black eyes. Determined eyes. "I want him dead. If I can get him alive, that will be better. And I will pay extra for the honor of disposing of him myself. I will pay to see him suffer."

Seconds or minutes must have passed, and I said nothing.

"I don't..." I wasn't sure what to say. *Be reasonable, Rashid? Vengeance isn't good for the soul, Rashid? Don't turn to the dark side? Don't get revenge for the death of your only son?*

Outliving your child is madness. It is wrong and unnatural in every possible way. It is the single greatest human tragedy that could happen. No one ever deserves to see the death of their child.

"How much?" he asked me.

"How much for what?"

"To get him. Dead or alive. I do not care. How much?"

I was dumbfounded. "I'm not...a hitman. I work security. I protect. I don't..."

"For fuck's sake, man, you know how to kill. You know how to capture," he hissed through gritted teeth. "You might not be a murderer, but you are a capable killer!" His meaty palm slammed down on his desk so hard, I thought the wood would splinter. "I know you can do this. I know more of your record than what you put on your company website. So how much?"

"I'm not a killer for hire." I fiddled with the glass in my hand and concentrated on its scent to keep me calm. Sherry. Oak. A slight hint of honey and caramel. The burn of alcohol.

"A million?" he said.

My head jerked up. That was far more than I charged. While my family assets kept up the cost of the castles in Scotland and financed several charities, the money from Caledonia Security was a different pot of money entirely. Never the twain shall meet. That kind of injection of funds would ensure more staff, better equipment, and an expansion.

"Ten million?"

This was not the man I knew. This wasn't the person who I had broken bread and shared drinks with over the past decade. It was the same flesh, the same body. But the sheer malice that radiated from his expressionless face was a stranger to me. Then there was that voice again, whispering in my brain; *You don't even know who you're protecting, do you?*

I placed the glass of scotch down and rose to my feet. I'd had enough. This conversation needed to end before this man, in his grief, did something irreparable.

"I'll see what I can do," I told him. Non-committal, no promises. "You know that I will always give you my utmost."

"See that you do." His expression closed off, blank.

On that unsettling note, I left.

I was silent as I took a taxi to the airport.

I was silent when I got on my private plane to Glasgow.

There was more silence as I picked up my Rolls-Royce, and white-knuckled back to the country house in Strathlachlan.

I couldn't settle my nerves until the large Tudor home, with plaster walls and intricate diamond paned glass came into view. English gardens with stone fountains and bird baths surrounded the estate. It harkened back to the days of King James V, before the Hanoverians took over the island.

Just seeing those rough back roads allowed the tension to leave my body.

There was something enormous and ancient about being a part of this land. I loved the rolling acres of highlands, and the cold air that came from the water. The land feels uninhabited, as if man was both an intruder and the participant in an ancient existence.

The wheels crunched on the cobblestone driveway before I entered the detached garage. Several cars backed into parking spaces; a habit formed during military service.

I glanced at Alastair's Aston Martin, Hugo's Jeep Wrangler, and Geordie's fully electric Mercedes-Benz EBQ-Class. There was also a Toyota Hilux, a truck that we used when doing labour around the estate.

I walked into the house through heavy, paned wooden double doors. It opened to a marble staircase on one side, and a great hall just beyond. The walls were covered in tapestries and ornate wooden panels, telling more of the house's long history than the portraits that covered its high halls.

The portraits dated back to Holbein, from the sixteenth century, all the way to the large oil portrait of me before I was shipped to St. Michael's.

What the hell am I doing with my life?

I went up the marble stairs. Around the narrow upstairs corridors were small apartments where the lads of Caledonia Security stayed. Even with the four of us in residence, there were still a dozen empty suites waiting to be occupied.

The silence was deafening when the lads weren't here.

The Master suite had once belonged to my parents. They inherited the furniture from my father's parents. Now it was bequeathed to me. There was something profoundly wrong about replacing any of the furniture, which included an ornate, hand-carved four-poster bed.

When my parent's received control of this house, they were newlyweds. When it was my turn, I was far away, in the service, and unable to come home.

I placed a hand in my pocket and looked up at the room's focal point.

A large oil painting of my parents hung on the wall across from the bed. My father stood sternly behind my mother as she sat primly on a high-back, red chair which could still be found in the downstairs library. My father's hand lay possessively on my mother's bare shoulder, and her own fingers reached up and grazed that hand as she smiled warmly.

They were very young in that portrait. I didn't have many memories of them as I rarely spent time in this house past infancy. This portrait was done shortly after their wedding, long before I was a reality. I wasn't overcome by a sense of loss when I looked them.

Instead, I felt a longing for normalcy. I didn't have Christmases with family who laughed around a tree. I didn't have a mother who kissed my scraped knee and wiped my tears away. My father never took the time to teach me things about manhood.

My memories were of nannies. then teachers and headmasters in stuffy suits in a crowded boy's dormitory in Switzerland.

I didn't spend much time in this bedroom. I slept on the couch in the library, surrounded by the smell of book bindings and leather, across from a bar full of whiskey decanters and red wine.

This was home. And home was where I did my best planning.

I fortified myself for the task ahead.

Time to go see the lads.

CHAPTER ELEVEN

Strathlachlan, Scotland

THE OLD WOODEN CARRIAGE house was renovated into the Caledonia headquarters. The brick walls were reinforced. The ceiling was covered with material to prevent incoming and outgoing wireless signals. The windows were blacked out and replaced with bulletproof glass.

The Caledonia offices were accessed by retinol scan. Only the four of us could go in unaccompanied. The large, hollow space was warm, humming with the sound of computers and monitors, and the light tapping of keys. Four cubicles nestled in each corner, the monitors facing the center of the room. A large mahogany conference table held the tea and coffee station and was used for our meetings.

When they heard me step in, Hugo's dark head popped up like a lemur and he pursed his lips.

"George said you were healed," his French accent was as thick as ever, "But you still look like shit."

"I can't imagine why the French aren't known for their charm." Alastair rolled his eyes; his dry flat BBC pronunciation elicited a chuckle from me.

"We may not be charming," Hugo sneered. "But at least our food isn't shit."

I smiled at them as we all moved to the large conference table.

"A'right, man?" Geordie asked softly, dropping into a seat.

"Aye, I'm a'right," I sighed, responding to his Scottish brogue with more of the same. "But I think I have problem."

I explained Rashid's request and how much he's willing to pay. To their credit, they listened silently without interrupting.

"We could put it to a vote, I suppose," said Geordie, shrugging.

"Ah, democracy," said Hugo. "A French concept."

"I don't think a vote is necessary," Alastair said. "Callum's right. We're not hitmen."

"What do you mean?" Hugo exclaimed. "We kill people all the time!"

"For the interest of security, yes," Alastair prevaricated. "We just don't kill for the sake of it."

"Maybe you don't," Hugo grumbled under his breath. "But we should."

"Is it really the same if we're targeting an assassin?" Geordie countered, ignoring Hugo.

"He stabbed me in the neck, but he didn't kill me," I said, getting up from my seat and heading to my cubicle at the north side of the room. "He could have pulled out the scalpel, and I would have bled to death. He could have slashed my throat. Instead, he signaled an S-O-S."

"Are we quite certain that was him?" Alastair asked.

"Who else could it be?" I countered.

Alastair grunted in acknowledgment; Hugo nodded. Geordie crossed his arms and raised a brow. They had been contemplating that little mystery, too. No doubt, Geordie filled them all in on what happened.

"Do we think that Junior was really a trafficker?" Hugo flicked his thumb at his computer. "We have found nothing to confirm this."

"I cannae find anything concrete," said Geordie. "At the rate he was going to brothels, and if you look at his travel...maybe?"

"So that's inconclusive." Alastair rose from his seat to make himself a cup of tea. "We would need more information, then, before we decide to become executioners."

"No." I went to my cubicle on the North side of the room. "I would be the executioner. I would not put that on you lads." I brought up the picture of Leonard Bonifacio. "It was my fault, so I would be the one to fix it."

"Oh, how delightfully noble." Alastair smiled sardonically, playing with the string of his earl gray tea bag.

I needed to know if the Ferryman was a force for good or if he was just another soulless, lethal mercenary. I could kill a psychopath, but not someone with a sense of morality. Not until I knew if they were on the side of the angels or devils.

"How hard could it be to kill a man who lives with their parents?" Hugo leaned back in his chair.

"You'd have to make sure not to kill the parents," Alastair said, blandly. "Or the sister, for that matter.

"Bah! The sister sounds like she's in on it anyway." His voice dripped with derision. Or maybe that was just his accent and his Parisian shrug. "Kill her, too."

"Have we found any more on the sister?" I didn't know if I asked because I wanted more information, or if I wanted to see her face again.

I turned to Geordie, my hackles rising at the mention of killing a woman. Of killing her. *Leanora.* The old-fashioned name didn't suit the woman with such a trendy pixie haircut.

Geordie got up and went to his monitors. Her picture came up on the screen.

God, she's gorgeous.

I didn't think that when I first saw her in Montreaux, but the more I studied that face, the more it etched into my brain as the most beautiful thing I'd ever laid eyes on. Strong. Mysterious.

Geordie flicked to other photos from social media. There were a series of photos of her in a blue bikini running into the water with a surfboard. Her small breasts, defined arms, and narrow hips were tense under the awkward weight of her short board. She was lean, powerful and supple, attacking the huge waves.

And that arse was something carved by the heavens.

In another photo, she was in a plain, black dress. It covered her from neck to mid-thigh. She held a drink in a tulip glass. Her brow arched and one side of her lip tipped up to show a hint of a smile.

Under her sweet face was an undertone of deviousness. Just the thought of that made me bite my lip.

I wanted to see her. I *needed* to see her again. Did she know that her brother was a killer? Did he tell her? Or was it a secret that he kept for himself?

Then again, every man in this room was a killer. Even me. We didn't advertise it to our nearest and dearest. No, I needed to look him in the eyes to determine if he needed a bullet to the head.

"I need to meet them." I made up my mind, coming to my feet to walk towards Geordie.

"Do you have a plan, then?" Alastair inquired, leaning back in his computer chair.

"Aye." I smiled at Geordie. "You said the family were devout Catholic."

Geordie's eyes narrowed, then widened in amusement. "Are ye gonna be a Father Ted, then? Do I get to come too?" he asked in a thick brogue. "I wouldn't mind sightseeing down in Hollywood. Maybe go see Sean Connery's star on Hollywood boulevard."

"Aye, maybe we could have some fun, "I let my Scottish accent get thick as mud. "Give me all the information you have on them. I want to crawl so far up their arse, they can floss with my shoelace."

"Done! We can go over everything on the flight," Geordie responded in kind, smacking his palms together and rubbing them in excitement. "I've never been to America."

"Are they really going to talk like that?" Hugo lamented to Alastair. "They're always impossible to understand with all their grunting and throat clearing. It's an abomination of a language."

CHAPTER TWELVE

"NANAY! I'M HOME!" I yelled as I came in the front door, toeing off my shoes and putting on my tsinelas; the cheap rubber sandals we wear indoors.

"*Anak!* You're late!" My mother yelled back from the dining room. I heard her chattering away to someone. An unknown man. Probably one of the many strays that got invited over for dinner.

My brother stood in the dining room archway; his arms crossed. He turned his head to look at me. His eyes looked... disturbed. He tilted his head towards the dining room table. It was a warning, telling me that whatever was about to happen, I would hate.

"We have a guest, Anak," Nanay said proudly, waving her hand to gesture me to the dining room as she moved toward the kitchen. The smell of her sinigang, a sour tamarind soup, wafted into the dining room.

At the table, with a cup of tea in front of him, was a man in a black suit. He was tall. Far too tall for furniture picked out by a family that averaged 5'6". His red hair was slicked back, curled at the nape. His matching beard was trim and square. He looked at me with mischievous green eyes.

When no one was looking, he smiled.

Checkmate, that smile said. Then his mask of reverent kindness returned.

It was him. He wasn't on some funeral pyre in Scotland, or whatever it was those people did for their dead Lords. He was very much alive and drinking my mother's tea.

And he *knew* who we were.

"You can't blame this one on me dropping a fork," I hissed at my brother. "This is un-fucking-believable."

"We need to increase security in this house," my brother said under his breath.

"We don't have security in the house," I whispered back.

The bodyguard was blowing on his tea to cool it down. The cup was dwarfed in his enormous hand.

"That's my point." He gestured as though he was smacking his palm on his forehead but didn't actually land it, so it didn't make a sound. "We should start."

Leo and I casually split up and took a spot on each side of this intruder. We flanked him in case he decided to do anything... irregular.

I took a seat beside the man, and Leo took the chair across from him. It meant that either of us could attack him at any moment without fear of crossing paths and getting in each other's way. We casually leaned our elbows on the table, ready to jump on him.

He smiled, completely nonchalant, giving us nothing but a brief raise of a quizzical brow.

"This is Father Deacon Callum," Nanay yelled from the kitchen. "He's new to the church."

I could hear my father shuffling in the living room, flipping channels.

"*Father* Callum, is it?" I asked, incredulous. I finally noticed the white square at his neck. Leaning toward him, I whispered too low for anyone else to hear, "Not Lord, Major or Special Agent?"

My mother came back into the dining room and gave me an annoyed look. "What are you whispering about? You better not be rude to a padre..."

"Father Deacon, if you please," Callum interrupted her, raising a hand, palm out in a supplicating gesture. "I'm not ordained as a priest yet."

He didn't have that off-putting American accent anymore. He was Scottish. Like William Wallace Scottish. He smiled towards me, and his eyes scanned me from head to toe. I sat up straight. It didn't make my skin crawl the way Brett did. It had a very different effect on me. An effect that I wasn't ready to analyze.

"Are you in seminary?" I was touching the balisong in my pocket, itching to bring it out and swing it in front of his Anglo nose.

"Yes." Callum had no fear in his eyes. He oozed friendliness and gentility with his light Scottish brogue. "I was just in Argentina before I got the invitation to help here. Who can resist the lure of California?"

"I didn't know that our church needed the help," Leo was trying not to grit his teeth in irritation.

Leo and Callum made eye contact. Their eyes tensed into slits, then relaxed. Their hands opened, fingers flexed and ready for any provocation. I took a deep breath. I forced myself to calm down too, one finger at a time, closing my eyes for a moment to bring my mask back down.

I am a fluffy, happy, carefree bunny.

"All help is good," Tatay turned off the television and entered the dining room. "And it's good that you come out to meet all the parishioners."

Tatay gave Leo a pointed glare, warning him not to be rude to our guest.

"Aye, I love to meet new people." Those green eyes turned back to me. "Though I can't help feeling like I've met you before." Those eyes were so warm, like the sun peeking through a canopy of leaves. "Have either of you traveled much recently?"

"They were in Argentina!" Nanay said excitedly, as she placed the pot of sinigang on the table, then went back to retrieve the bowl of steaming white rice. He was staying for dinner, of course. My parents would have insisted. No guest was ever allowed to leave our house hungry. That's not the Filipino way.

Nanay and Tatay took their customary seats at the heads of the table.

Leo was trying to hide his hostility while still posturing. He stared at Callum and squared his shoulders to rise as tall as his 5'8 would allow him. It was as if his restrained tension traveled through the air and jolted into me as well.

"Argentina?" Callum smiled at me, feigning surprise. God, that accent was doing things to me. "I have some mixed feelings about that place. I had a little accident and ended up needing to go to hospital. I hurt my shoulder very badly." He put his hand where I stabbed him and started rotating his arm. "But I'm all mended now. Maybe we were there at the same time. When were you there?"

Leo and I looked at one another. I shook my head and refused to answer.

"Before that, I was in Switzerland," he continued when he got no response from us. "Have either of you been there?"

"I'm surprised that the church was taking on more staff." Leo's direct change of subject got a smile out of Callum.

"How would you know, Leo?" Nanay reprimanded. "You rarely ever go to church anymore. You only go when you're home and my ungrateful children are never home."

"Nanay!" Leo exclaimed in disbelief, his hands up at his sides, palms out in an astonished shrug.

But Callum didn't seem to care. He was relaxed. Intrigued, even. He was looking at Leo with complete fascination, like he was trying to figure him out and something wasn't clicking.

"So," Fluffy bunny me had to de-escalate this. I pitched my voice high and plastered on a fake smile. Leo was ready to throw a knife into his throat. We can't do that in front of our parents. "What brings you over to us for dinner?"

I smelled that cologne again. The trees and forest smell. Maybe he was a lumberjack in his spare time. He turned towards me, and his green eyes seemed to brighten. "I was just going through the neighborhood when Ligaya invited me in for dinner."

It was off-putting hearing my mother's name. My heart clenched.

"Did you meet our other neighbors?" Leo asked in a sharp, clipped tone.

Callum flinched in surprise, as if he'd been distracted. He turned quickly back to him, breaking our eye contact. Leo heaped the soup over a bowl of white jasmine rice. The cooked, green spinach decorated the top of his bowl like garnish, and succulent tender pork scented the air around us. My parents were digging in, leaving me and Callum with empty plates.

I took Callum's bowl and gave him a serving before taking some for myself, knowing that guests weren't always accustomed to this family style. It was polite to accommodate them. That's what a fluffy bunny would do. Hospitality is the Filipino way.

Callum's large forearm grazed the table as he shifted to look at me. He knocked a fork from the white linen tablecloth, and it clattered to the floor between the two of us. Leo and I stared at where his utensil had been.

Callum bent down to pick it up. He paused and took a deep breath as he leaned towards me. He looked up as if he was seeing me for the first time.

As if he recognized me.

Our mother reached out, insisting on getting him a clean one even as Callum protested, saying that a little bit of dirt wouldn't kill him. The doorbell rang.

Leo and I rolled our eyes and groaned.

"*Hoy!*" our father chastised, getting up from his seat, "You two will be polite. This is my house; we are good hosts to all guests." Our mother and father got up to answer the door.

Duly chastised, Leo and I crossed our arms and legs and frowned.

I tilted my head towards Callum, and grumbled to Leo, "Just so you know, this is *his* fault." I pointed at where Callum had dropped his fork.

Callum raised an eyebrow, one corner of his mouth tilted up and he looked at me. He was amused. Confused, but amused.

"Definitely your fault," Leo said quietly to Callum. The giant man turned his attention to my brother, then looked back at me again. His eyes glinted and wrinkled on the edges like he was trying not to smile.

We heard Brett Bradley's voice carry down from the foyer, around the hall and, finally, to us in the dining room like a cloud of annoying doom.

"Listen." I leaned ever so slightly towards Callum. He smelled so good. Earthy and woodsy. "If you're here to kill us, leave our parents out of it. But...make sure you kill this fucking guy, too."

Leo snorted. Callum smiled. He beamed.

It was a good smile, though. It didn't just reach his eyes, but his entire body. Good lord. He felt with his entire being.

I sat straight in my chair, turning my eyes away from him and looking at the Jesus on the cross.

But he wasn't done with me. He tilted towards me until I felt his breath on my ear. "You think I'm here to hurt you?"

He seemed genuinely concerned that I would think that. I pulled away from him, and examined his face, the relaxed placement of his hands, the tilt of his head...

there were no signs of deception. He wasn't going to hurt us. At least not right now.

I felt him inhale again. Was he...smelling me? He stared at my face, not my body, which should have been a relief to me, but it wasn't. Had he looked at my body, or even scanned the length of my halter, I would have understood. But he didn't. He was looking right into my eyes and if I didn't know any better, I'd say he felt...lust?

He took another breath, like he was a wolf sniffing the air for prey. His head tilted, and he leaned back into his chair.

What was he thinking? What was going on behind that handsome face?

"Get away from my sister." Leo was leaning with his elbows on the table, glaring at the man.

My brother wasn't frowning, but his brow was creased. His eyes were laser-focused, narrowed, but his face was placid. Calm. That was his killing face.

When Leo caught my gaze, his expression told me *this guy is a fucking psycho.*

My eyes told him that I agreed.

Our mother, father and Brett came into the dining room the way a bull comes into a China shop. Loud, obnoxious, and unable to read the room.

Brett was on a roll, as always. Talking, talking and *talking*. "It's been a great week for me. I've got a great feeling about this. It's important to get in at the ground floor, you know? Get in nice and early. That's how rich people invest..."

"Hey Brett," Leo said loudly, interrupting him, with an uncommon bite to his tone. "How's it going with that fake money?"

Silence. More silence. It was heavy and steamy like a fresh dump.

"Leo!" I said, kicking him under the table. My sibling looked back at me with a mischievous grin.

My parent's mouths hung open, flabbergasted by his rudeness. Callum's eyes bounced between all of us. He bit his lips, trying to hide a smile again and failing.

"Leo, you know that NFTs aren't just made-up money," Brett sputtered. There was an uncharacteristic hesitation in his voice when he caught a glimpse at Callum, but he soon recovered. He droned on about bitcoin, the economy, and his tokens. None of it required audience participation.

Really? I mouthed to my brother across the table, who was grinning.

He shrugged. *What?* he mouthed back.

I rolled my eyes. I glanced at Callum again. His eyes were looking between me and my brother like he was watching a Wimbledon match.

"I haven't been this amused in years," Callum said through his lopsided smile. Then he looked me up and down. His smile broadened even further.

Un-fucking-believable. He was laughing at *me*. Oh, how the tables have turned.

"I will actually be pissed," I whisper-snarled at him, low enough that only he could hear, "if you don't kill this guy, too."

Callum guffawed. It was a glorious sound. Full-bodied and genuine. It made my mother smile. My dad even grinned a little. Brett tried to join in the laughter as if he was in on the joke, too. Only Leo and I stayed silent, shocked.

Brett started talking to Tatay about his NFT's again. My mom chimed in with mm-hmms, nods and words of affirmation like "that's so interesting" or "Wow! I didn't know that!"

They were her standard polite replies to show that she was listening, even though she sometimes wasn't.

"Il est fou," Leo said to me in French. *He's crazy.* I nodded in agreement, unsure which of our guests he meant. It worked for both. Our parents didn't speak French, so it was our default when keeping secrets. And there were a lot of secrets to be had around this household.

"Only English at the table!" Tatay ordered us, then went back to listening to Brett.

Callum cleared his throat and adjusted his collar and said in a low voice, "I assure you, I'm not here for any... killing. You have my word."

"We have your word as a clergyman?" Leo's sarcasm would be lost on the innocent parties at the table, but the three of us understood it.

"On my immortal soul," Callum was smiling, raising his hand as if in a pledge. Then he turned to me and winked. What the shit? Was he flirting with me? No way.

But it didn't make my stomach turn. I didn't have to fight a grimace of disgust. I liked it. I liked his attention.

He *knew* me. Not the fluffy bunny persona that I kept for the world. He knew *me* as the Ferryman. I could knock him on his ass – and I *did!* – and he was still attracted to me? That had never happened before. None of the boys in school or the blind dates that came in adulthood ever knew me. I knew that they'd flee. But this guy...pursued.

"Oh, is anyone going to introduce me?" Brett's unwelcome voice broke into my thoughts and brought the whole table into the same conversation again. "I'm Brett Bradley, I live next door." He put out his hand towards Callum.

"I'm Father Deacon Callum MacLachlan."

The two shook hands. Brett tried to hide the wince when Callum's paw clapped over his.

"Well, that's a mouthful," Brett laughed. "Since you're a church guy, I'll forgive you for taking my seat. Usually, I'm the one who sits by Lea." Brett winked at me.

I winced. This was the second guy to wink at me today. *What the hell is happening? Is a planet in retrograde?*

Brett dropped into the seat by Leo, continuing to smile at me. I didn't smile back.

"Is that right?" Callum's eyebrow rose again. He looked over at me. I shook my head. If I'm going to die, I refuse to die with anyone – including my killer – thinking that I am somehow romantically involved with *that* asshole. That's a level of embarrassment no one deserves.

"Yeah, that's right," Brett said. "Lea and I go way back."

Callum's eyebrow rose in disbelief.

"He means," I interject, flattening my hand on the table and leaning in, "he's been our neighbor for several years."

"Yeah but...you know...we've been out a few times." Brett waggled his eyebrows, implying that there was something else there. "Anyway, I was just telling your dad that I was getting into CrossFit."

Of course, he was. Of-fucking-course he was going to be into CrossFit. There wasn't a trend or fad that Brett wouldn't latch on to.

Brett continued to speak, and I inhaled, tuning him out. As the meal progressed, I could feel Callum's eyes on the side of my face, heating my skin. I tried to ignore his existence. I pushed my food around, just trying to get through this.

I checked back into the conversation right as Brett said, "And I've never felt so manly in my life. I mean, I'm as potent as a bumble bee. Bet you've never done anything like that, have you, Father Callum?"

Jesus Christ, I missed something. Was he seriously trying to emasculate a man of God? Sure, he was a *fake* man of God, but Brett didn't know that.

"Anything like what, exactly? Being potent?" Callum antagonized him with an arched brow. Lord help me, but I kind of liked that.

"I mean...anything that manly! Primal fitness is about waking the warrior within," Brett insisted, pounding his chest twice. "I mean, you're a man of God and all that, so you're all about peace and celibacy, right?"

I sometimes had to bask in the complete and utter un-reality that Brett lived in. He waded through his entire life completely ignorant and unaware of anything and everything that was happening around him. It was a level of masculine naivete that was both annoying, and enviable.

"He was in the Special Air Service," Leo glared at Callum. "Weren't you, *Father Deacon?*" He said the man's title with complete derision.

"How do you know that?" Nanay said, sounding surprised. "Also, what is that?"

Callum chuckled. He was taunting my brother. "What gave me away?"

"I don't know. Something in your manner." Leo was projecting a threat, posturing, letting him know that whatever he had up his sleeve, we could counter. Whatever information he had on us, we had on him as well.

I couldn't tell if Callum received the message.

"Oh, is that like the Irish Air Force?" Brett chimed in.

I shut my eyes and took a deep, cleansing breath. Jesus, *Brett, shut the fuck up before you hurt yourself.*

"I'm Scottish," Callum said, without looking away from Leo, though the explanation was for everyone else at the table. "And it's the British Special Forces. You seem very well informed, Leo."

"Yes!" Nanay beamed. "They're very smart. When they were kids, the two of them would start babbling to each other. I thought they just had their own special language. You know, because they're twins! But it turned out that they decided to learn French, or Chinese, or Swedish. So they'd only talk to each other in that language until they were fluent. So clever!" Nanay's smile faded as she looked at her precious boy. "I don't know why he doesn't go back to school to become a doctor." It wasn't lost on me that only Leo could become a doctor. "Maybe even settle down, give me grandchildren to take care of. Maybe you can convince him, padre! And also Lea! It's time she settles down, too." My mother nodded ever so slightly towards Brett, as though he was a candidate for such partnership.

I thought running into my target's bodyguard was bad. But no. This. This very situation was the absolute worst thing that could possibly happen to anyone, *ever*.

My face turned red. My ears were burning. I was about to lose it.

"Absolutely, they should give you grandchildren. Children are a gift from God." Callum was staring at me again. *Asshole.*

I needed to escape. I shot up to my feet and looked at Leo. His brow creased, trying to figure out my play.

"I'm gonna get the desserts," I chirped, smiling like a fluffy bunny. I picked up my used plate before gathering up my father's, then Brett's.

"I'll help you." Callum got up and started piling up the remaining plates and utensils. I reached out to grab his pile and he pulled it out of my reach.

Fuck. I looked at Leo. His eyes widened in fear. I looked back at Callum. His smile was unwavering. He nodded for me to lead the way to the kitchen.

Out of the corner of my eye, I saw my brother shake his head.

Don't go, his expression told me. I was frozen, looking at my parents. Then my brother. Then back at the smiling Scotsman. Was his jovial routine just a ruse? Was he really here to get me alone and slit my throat?

I can take him out, right?

I had a weapon. My knife was in my back pocket. I could get the drop on him.

If I killed him in the kitchen, though, how would I get him out? How would I dump the body? What would I tell my parents? Would I need to clean blood from the floor? Fuck!

I didn't have a plan. I needed a plan.

If he tried to come after me, I could strike the carotid. He'd bleed out in seconds. I could get between his ribs. The third intercostal space, and I could hit his lung. That would require less clean up. If I'm behind, I could get a kidney. If I can manage to get the inner thigh, I can get his artery. He'd die fast. But it'd be a mess. How would I explain that? And he didn't seem like he wanted to hurt us.

No, I won't kill him. Not yet. But I will make the first move and find out why he's here. That's it. I need to put him on the defense.

"Let your sister and the padre go." That was our father's authoritative voice. "You two can be separated for a few minutes."

Leo was paralyzed. He wanted to defy our parents, but he didn't know how. I wanted him to stay where he was. To stay safe. To protect our family. I shook my head, and with my eyes pointed to his chair, telling him to sit back down.

"Ne t'inquète pas, cheri," that Scottish voice said. His native accent was so thick, it took a while to realize he was speaking in French. "Je ne mords pas."

Don't worry, darling. I don't bite.

So, he speaks French, too. I should have known. He did go to school in Switzerland, after all. It had just slipped my mind.

So much for the element of surprise.

CHAPTER THIRTEEN

It was satisfying to watch the two of them pale.

I was sure they thought I was getting her alone for nefarious reasons. I wasn't. I came here to get more information. I stayed because I was drawn to her. To her smell, her wit.

Now, I was snooping, trying to find out more about her life.

When I arrived at the house, their mother, Ligaya, invited me in right away. She was obviously a religious woman, as evident by the large crucifix hanging in their dining room. She beamed with pride when she spoke about her twins, even as she listed their failings.

Then Leo arrived, kicking off one pair of leather sandals and replacing them with smaller plastic ones. He spent his morning surfing. His hair was still damp and matted with salt and sand. He looked horrified that I was sitting with their mom at the dinner table. She wanted me to meet all of her children, of course, and insisted I drink some tea and have dinner with them. I gladly accepted as Leo watched me from the hallway.

Leo glared at me from the hallway until my woman arrived. She absentmindedly kicked off her climbing shoes at the door and donned on similar plastic sandals. Her tight-fit leggings and halter hid nothing of her taut body. I could see every sinew and tendon with her movements, and it went straight to my cock.

She had a light sheen of sweat, her little platinum hair plastered to her forehead and around her jaw. I wanted to make her sweat, then taste her on my tongue. I wanted to see her head roll back in ecstasy as I bit into her neck and marked her with my teeth.

That thought was so intrusive, I needed to literally shake it out of my head, and cough to get rid of the lump that formed in my throat.

When the two of them stood together, they didn't look real. They were identical, barring their gender and a difference of a few inches in height. Their stance, their posture, the way they held their muscular shoulders were the same. They were impressive physical specimens, not an ounce of fat on either of them, and they moved with synchronicity that could only come from a lifetime of proximity.

My eyes kept drifting to her. For all their similarities, there was something about her, and it wasn't just that she was an attractive woman.

I was obsessed.

This family had a closeness that left me with a pang of envy. They moved around each other with a familiarity that was so... routine. The last dinner I had with my parents was in a formal setting, in suits, with four courses and brandy. I never had siblings, but if I had, would I be close like these two? Probably not. Twins were a level of closeness that I'd never understand.

With dirty plates in hand, Lea led the way to the kitchen. She walked like she was heading for a firing squad, her shoulders tense, her held head high. If she was going to go, she was going to go out with dignity.

But I decided that I could not be an executioner. Especially not hers. I could say she was beautiful, and that I was enamored. But that wasn't it. I could see the dark bags under her eyes, the unevenness of her pallor. Her hair tangled at the edges. Her hands were hardened, her knuckles were tough with dried callouses. She even had the slightest veins visible on her forearms – the vascularity a sign of physical strength that was unusual in a woman.

And fuck me, that was incredibly attractive.

She didn't need protection from violence. A man didn't have to hide his gun or refrain from speaking about the horrors of their job with a woman like her. A man like me wouldn't need to hide the violence that existed in the fabric of my being because she was cut from the exact same cloth.

The moment I got a hint of that perfume... the moment it clicked that *he* wasn't the killer, but *she* was, I knew that I would protect her.

It was mad, but she was a woman so rare in this world that I needed to keep her, to have her.

A deeper part of me—a part I did not want to acknowledge—wanted to possess her, too. I intuitively knew that she'd be the kind of woman to scratch and bite and grind with the same violence of action that she did everything else. Would she fuck the way she sparred? I was willing to find out.

When the kitchen door swung shut, she dropped the plates in the sink. I did the same, coming in close to and hovering behind her. That floral perfume enveloped me again.

The quiet was shattered by a metal clink as the woman deftly turned, an unsheathed butterfly knife clutched in her palm. The long, slim blade glinted in the yellow overhead light.

She stopped its movement right above my clavicle, threatening to cut through my shirt and into my skin.

"Careful, darling," I said with a smirk. "Haven't you already tried to stab me there? I don't think it will bode that well for you this time either."

We were only centimeters apart. I could see every refraction as her eyes dilated.

"If I wanted to kill you, you'd be dead." Her snarl was low, almost a whisper. "Let's not pretend that I didn't leave you alive on purpose."

"Why did you?" I pushed my shoulder into her blade, and she pulled it back, unwilling to cut my skin. That made me smile.

"Because I wasn't there for you." She sneered as though it was the most obvious thing in the world.

I stepped forward again, daring her to cut me with her blade. She stepped back in response. I took another, slower step. She held her ground, but the pressure of the blade never changed over my black shirt, until I could feel the heat of her tiny body.

"No collateral damage. Is that part of your reputation true, darling?"

"Stop calling me that," she gritted out.

"What? Darling?" I let the endearment roll smoothly from my lips in my natural brogue. She softened, obviously liking my voice. "That particular term suits a bonnie wee thing like you...*darling*."

I saw her top lip curl in scorn, her brow creased. Her brown eyes burned with malice.

I decided that one day, not only would I call her sweet endearments, but that she would respond in kind.

"Why are you here, asshole?" she hissed.

"To see you, Atalanta," I said in a low, husky growl. Her eyes widened in shock. Ah, so she did remember me. Did I inhabit her thoughts the way she had mine? "We didn't finish our conversation when you so rudely stabbed me." I reached out to encircle the slim wrist of the hand that held the blade. It was so small that my fingers and thumb overlapped. Her skin was cold, her hands strong, her long, elegant fingers were calloused. "We should get the dessert before your boyfriend wonders what we're doing in here."

"I only murder for money," she hissed through gritted teeth, "but if you call Brett my boyfriend again, I'll make you my first recreational kill."

I let out a laugh. It wasn't the reaction she wanted. She looked annoyed, which made me laugh more.

"So, you're single then?" I finally asked.

"Really? That's what you focused on? Not the *I'm going to kill you* part?" She was delightfully exasperated. "There really isn't enough blood for both heads, is there?"

I shrugged. "I'll show you one day, darling."

I reached up and lightly ran my fingers over her tensed jaw. When she didn't flinch, I cupped her cheek. She didn't have a strong cheekbone. Her cheeks, forehead and nose were quite flat, which made her plump lips her most dominant feature. I ran my thumb over her lower lip, and they parted on a small gasp. But she wasn't aroused. She looked astonished by my audacity.

"You won't kill me in your parents' kitchen," I told her.

It was a statement, not a question. I know she would rather die than bring their dubious occupation home with her. Her love for them was clear as day.

"You won't kill me in my parents' kitchen," she echoed back to me. Clever girl.

"Aye, I won't."

Even though I knew that she was a killer, she still seemed precious. She was tiny, barely reaching my shoulder. That fierce visage didn't have a stitch of makeup and it made her look even younger. As far as covers, her very being was a good one. I would never have suspected that she'd be a cold-blooded killer.

I reminded myself that it didn't matter what she looked like or how tiny she was. No matter how intoxicating her scent, she was a killer. Not to be underestimated. And yet...

"What's your perfume?" I leaned in just a touch, tilting my head down towards her neck so I could get that fragrance again. I closed my eyes to fully enjoy it.

"Filipino jasmine." Her voice was a whisper. Whatever resolve she had was waning. "*Sampaguita.*"

Jasmine. Pale, delicate and sweet. It was so unlike her but also fitting. The plant itself was resilient, able to survive in many climates could scale it's way to the sky.

Maybe that was my obsession. She had grit. She had bite, and spirit. She was a woman that could tear a man apart with a flick of her wrist. To have a woman like that surrender to me...it would only be on her terms, with her enthusiastic consent.

Fuck that was sexy.

"I won't hurt you," I promised her. "At least not tonight."

Her blade hand relaxed. She let me push it from my shoulder. I never released her hand, enjoying the feel of being joined in this dangerous tango.

"Then what do you want from me?"

"A little understanding, love." I smiled when her nose wrinkled at the endearment. "And for you to meet me for drinks. Tomorrow. We have to talk."

I pulled away and took a card and pen from my pocket. I scrawled on it before slipping it into the front pocket of her leggings where a phone could be kept. The back of my hand grazed against the inner lining. On the other side of that lining was her skin. The delicate, soft skin of her pelvis.

I pulled away from her for my own sake. My body hummed with the need to have her bare beneath me.

"Meet me there, tomorrow at seven." My breathing was ragged, uneven. "We can finish our conversation alone."

I cleared my throat as I picked up a pile of small saucers and forks. I grabbed them, assuming they were the dessert plates.

"And if I don't?" her voice was quiet, barely a whisper.

"Let me be clear, darling." I came back to her, leaning over her until our foreheads almost touched. I knew I was being an arsehole. I felt it in my soul. The next words out of my mouth would make me feel like dirt. "I know who you are, where you live, and who your family is. This is not a request. It would be a mistake to treat it as such."

"You're threatening me." Another statement, not a question.

"No. I'm threatening *them*." I nodded my head towards the dining room, where her family sat.

She recoiled. "You wouldn't."

She's right. I wouldn't. But I needed her to believe that I would. This was the quickest way to bend her to my will.

"I'm not a priest," I bared my teeth. "You have no idea what my confessions are."

"What will it take for you to leave my family alone?"

That was all I needed to hear.

"Meet me tomorrow, and I'll tell you."

CHAPTER FOURTEEN

I COULDN'T SLEEP. I laid in my bed, tossing and turning. I should have been concerned and scared out of my mind. Instead, I was anxious, and not in an unpleasant way. I wanted to see him again, and I hated it.

In the morning, Leo and I researched the restaurant.

It was high-end, and exclusive. A place where everyone wore tuxes or gowns. Exactly the kind of place that kept the middle-class rabble like us away.

"You'll have to buy a dress," Leo said.

"No way. Where will I hide a gun?" I couldn't wear a gown. If women couldn't wear underwear in dresses because it caused lines, then there was no way I could hide a holster.

"You can carry a purse," Leo said as if it was the most obvious thing in the world.

I looked at the women on the restaurant's website. They were real patrons, enjoying real drinks. The kind so rich that they were all flawlessly beautiful. Some clearly had surgical help in that regard. I was out of my depth.

Maybe I should wear a dress. Not to impress Callum. No, that would be ridiculous. But to blend in.

I tried hundreds of dresses at the Outlet Mall. I eventually settled on a long-sleeved red gown that had pleats from my right shoulder, between my breasts, and diagonally to a slit at the top of my left thigh. Small pearls scattered below the bra line. It was wildly impractical, scratchy, and made of an un-breathable synthetic fabric. But it looked good, so it would work.

I purchased a black sequined clutch that fit a Walther PPK and added a pair of those knock off Louboutin shoes. They were the kind with red bottoms that all those rich people wore.

That evening, I put on red lipstick and slicked back my hair. I knew that this would be as good as it got for me.

Leo replaced one of the pearls under the bust line with a camera, and another with a microphone. The cables were taped to my torso that ran to a battery pack awkwardly taped near my inner thigh.

This was not something we did often. We weren't private investigators. We were assassins. But the movies made this look easy, so... we'd give it a shot.

When I looked in the mirror, I hated what I saw. It didn't look like me. I was playing dress up. I wasn't this person, and I must have looked as awkward as I felt.

"I don't like this," I whispered.

Leo continued to strap a gun into his waistband.

"I'll be in your ear the whole time." He untucked my hair from behind my ear to cover the earpiece. "Nothing is going to happen. Nothing bad *can* happen. And if it does, I'll be there."

"So we can die together? I'd rather you just stay out of it if that's the case."

He didn't react. He was down to business. My calculated, responsible brother.

Like always, we traveled separately. I took a taxi to the bar, and he followed five minutes later in the Audi. He stayed in the parking lot. He could get into the hotel bar within thirty seconds. Faster if he ran.

Barring a bullet to the head, I could fight anyone off for thirty seconds.

The lobby's floor was marble, accented with yellow flecks. Velvet red drapes framed large windows that looked towards the busy traffic. The color matched the bottom of my shoes. Everything was Art-Déco, with golden angular, patterned lines that were glossed to a high shine.

The doormen and concierge desk just beyond wore bell boy uniforms and stood erect at their stations, nodding politely at guests.

A hostess stood at a podium right outside the bar's glass and heavy wooden double doors. She wore a tight black dress and a severe ballerina bun. She tapped a red fingernail on a large podium, looking down her nose at casually dressed passersby. She barred the entrance of anyone who did not have a reservation.

I halted a few feet from her, gripping my clutch close to me. I took a deep breath. *Fluffy bunny. It's just another mission. And I am a fluffy, expensive, bunny.*

"*I'll be in your ear the whole time,*" Leo whispered into the earpiece. It was a small comfort.

The hostess looked me up and down. Her lips pursed as she decided that I was somehow wanting.

"Do you have a reservation?" her voice dripped with that non-regional, California perfection.

"It'll be under MacLachlan."

She pursed her lips and looked at me skeptically before she perused the list of names on her docket. I kept my smile wide and doe-eyed. *Because I am the fluffiest of dumb bunnies.*

"I don't think I see that name…"

She was interrupted by a low, rumbling voice that bellowed out from behind the oak and glass doors that swung open behind her. "Darling, you're here."

Callum was wearing a navy-blue suit and silver tie. His beard was shorter than it had been the day before. There was no priest's collar this time.

His smile was gentle as he reached a hand toward me. He oozed a certain enthusiasm and exuberance that I didn't expect. I put my hand in his and he pulled me to his side.

"Thank you, Chelsea," he said, giving the hostess a curt nod.

He walked me in with his arm tight around my waist. He leaned down and whispered, "You look spectacular."

His voice was British this time, just like how I remembered it.

"Is this your real voice?" I whispered as he led me to the booths with amber leather seats and shiny tabletops. He smiled but didn't answer me.

I was under dressed. The women wore perfect hair and makeup more suitable for a wedding than a bar. The men wore suits. That was rather unremarkable. All suits basically look the same. But the women looked like they were ready to storm a runway and I was ready for a prom in a school gymnasium.

At least my shoes were right, since I saw several women wearing them. Except, of course, they probably wore the real thing.

A few women looked at my dress in a condescending scan and pursed their lips in disapproval. The men looked at my face, my hair and body, and seemed to find something lacking there, too.

"Beautiful clutch," he said as his hand slid from my elbow down my forearm to the fingers clasping my purse in a death grip. "Looks heavy. You must be carrying. Let me guess... a Glock? No, a PPK." He grinned down at me. "Don't you trust me?"

"Of course not." My eyes narrowed. I turned my body towards him so that my upper arm would graze across his ribs and over his delicious, hard abs searching for his weapon. He leaned ever so slightly into my touch like a cat preening while it was stroked.

He didn't have a weapon there. No holster, and not even a wallet in his inner pocket.

"I wear it on my belt, near the back," he whispered into my ear, and I felt his breath on my cheek which spread goosebumps down my spine.

"Interesting choice," I cleared my throat.

He guided me to a booth near the center of the room with a direct view to the windows that opened to the outdoor seating.

"*He's packing. Acknowledged,*" Leo said into my ear.

"I find that it's less obvious and doesn't hurt the lines of my suit."

"Ah," I said, realizing. "So, it's all about the look."

He chuckled. "Looks are an important part of tradecraft, don't you think?"

"I don't know what you mean." That was the truth. I didn't know what he meant. I was a *real* nurse. I did real medical things. I just happened to drown or poison the occasional victim. There was no tradecraft necessary. I never pretended to be anyone else but who I was.

He offered me a hand as we came to the table, but I slid in without assistance. I watched as he unbuttoned his blazer before taking a seat across from me.

There was a TV near the bar. It was on a low volume, showing the news. Callisandra Davenport, her wild, frizzy mane flying in the wind, stood beside Alex Baas. They were in front of a tent, the Baas Medical logo proudly displayed on the white tarp. She thrust the microphone in his face, and he looked at her with a sheepish grin as he spoke. She smiled up at him, her mouth a little open, leaning forward as though she were a mouse stuck in the hypnotizing power of a serpent.

I wonder why he's not married to some super model or something? A guy who was single handedly guilting all rich people in the world to give to charity needed to have a bimbo wife. That was just the way the world balanced out. If he married a brilliant woman, then their kids would take over the world and reinstate the monarchy.

Maybe he'd end up with a Playboy Bunny. Yeah. That'd make sense.

"Alex has a way with women," Callum interrupted my thoughts. He was looking at the TV, then back at me. "He tends to leave women wide mouthed whenever he's near."

I realized that my mouth hung open. I closed it.

"I am positively jealous." He smiled, a glint of amusement in his eye.

"You know him?" I cleared my throat and looked down at the table. It was a red wood, glossed and with silver lines making the pattern of a rose.

"We went to boarding school together."

"Of course, you did." I snorted. "Of course, you're on a first name basis with one of the richest men in the world." He looked at me with his head tilted, waiting for me to go on. I decided to be honest. "I thought I was important because I heard him speak in person once. When I went to volunteer at his clinic in Kemet."

"Was that for your job, or...?"

"I was there for legitimate reasons. To help." My voice came out with more force than I intended. "I don't only kill people." *Don't give him more than what you have to.* "But people like you and Mr. Baas live in a different world than I do."

"It's not that different, I promise you," he whispered. Was he using conversation to lull me into a false sense of security? Like a farmer trying to gently slaughter a lamb? "What is your drink of choice?"

"I'm not picky."

"Everyone is picky." There was that lopsided smile again. "Tell me what you normally drink."

"I suppose, I drink whiskey." I shrugged.

He looked surprised. "Oh? You suppose?"

"If I must drink, yes. If I want to get drunk, I find it more economical."

He leaned back in his seat, crossed his arms, and looked at me. "Economical?"

"It gets me to a buzz sooner, and cheaper."

He blinked. Silence. Minutes passed, and he hadn't moved. He was considering something complex. I could practically see the hamster working overtime on the wheel inside his head.

"Are all your decisions so frugal?" he finally said, as he looked down at my clothes, then down to my shoes. Did everything about me scream cheap?

"Let me guess, you're so rich that money is no object?"

He grinned at my comment, then shrugged, unapologetically.

Of course, he's that kind of rich.

To try to puncture his ego, I said, "And obviously not self-made."

"Obviously." He chuckled, not embarrassed in the least.

"Anyway..." I rolled my eyes. "One kind of liquor isn't that different from another. The overpriced label doesn't make it taste better."

He looked offended. "You cannot believe that."

He raised a finger to a passing waiter with overladen arms. The waiter nodded at him in acknowledgment before finishing his delivery.

"I don't know where you got your shoes from." He reached around the table, his hand landing on my knee before his warm fingers went down my bare calf to my ankle. He brought my foot up, my heel resting on his knee. "But the real thing, the Louboutin, is handcrafted. Each one is inspected so the seams are impeccable and hidden, and it's made of leather, not whatever synthetic material these might be." His palm landed on the top of my foot before his fingers wrapped around my ankle. It was a possessive gesture, and I gasped at the intimacy. "Now, you're right. The reason they are thousands of dollars and not tens of dollars, is because of the label, but there is a quality difference there too. The value of that difference may be arbitrary, but it's there."

I pulled my leg back and tucked my shoes under the table, hiding them from his view.

The waiter arrived and Callum ordered a couple things I did not recognize before dismissing him. I didn't get to order anything. He was one of *those* guys. The kind that ordered for their dates... assuming that this was a kind-of date. That's a strike against him.

"But my noticing these things has nothing to do with how I perceive their value." He continued as if there was no interruption. "You look positively gorgeous. Your face is exquisite, and your body is..." He bit his lip for just a second, then let out a slight cough. "But you don't fit in here, and maybe people won't understand why. They'll just know it. Your dress is lovely on you, but it's not silk or satin. It doesn't move with you, and it's not tailored. The seams are careless. The pearls are clearly not real, and I can see that at least one of them doesn't match the others perfectly, so I'm guessing... you're wearing a camera?"

He looked at my face for an answer. I gave him none, but he acted as if I had confirmed his statement.

"The sequins on your clutch are glued, not sewn, on." He reached across the table and grabbed my hand, flipping it so it was palm down. "Your nails aren't painted. Nothing wrong with your nails being natural, but a woman that came here regularly would at least put a clear coat on there for some extra polish." His thumb lingered over the back of my hand, before letting go. I sheepishly brought my hand back to my lap. "So, if I knew nothing else about you – and mind you, I know a lot at this point – I would see that you are pretending to be something else, in a place you don't belong." He nodded to my clutch. "And you're armed. You, my darling, are a threat."

I blinked once. Twice. A third time.

I had been silent for a whole two minutes now and his gaze never wavered as he patiently waited for my response.

"You talk a lot," I told him.

He guffawed. It was an honest laugh of surprise and delight. He brought his hand to his mouth, and leaned his chin into his palm, tilting his head as he looked at me.

The waiter came by with a tray, balancing four glasses. He wordlessly placed them on the table and walked away.

"I watched it come from the bartender. Nothing funny in the glasses," Leo's disembodied voice whispered in my ear.

I hadn't even considered that Callum would do such a thing. Jesus, was I already trusting this guy? At least one Bonifacio twin was keeping their head on straight. As always, it wasn't me.

I reached out for the glass nearest to me. His paw shot out and with a quick flick, he slapped my hand away.

"What the fuck?" I said, louder than was proper.

I'm going to dump him overboard between here and Catalina Island. Asshole.

"No," he said, definitively. "This is an education in one of the most important things that you will ever need to know."

"More than how my clothes make me look poor?" Maybe I was pouting.

"More than that, yes."

CHAPTER FIFTEEN

Her face soured when I slapped her hand away. There was murder in her beautiful eyes, and it made me chuckle. She was a vicious, little beauty.

"A'right, lad, get that stupid look off your face," I could hear Geordie in my ear. He was outside on the restaurant's patio, looking into his phone, watching the feed from the camera in my tie pin. If he looked at the huge glass windows from his place outside, he could see directly into where we were seated. *"Ye're going the right way fur a skelpit dowp."* You're going the right way to smack bottom.

I don't know if I was smiling at her as much as I was smiling at Geordie's commentary.

He already called me an arse for telling her she looked poor. If she punched me in the face, he'd think I deserved it.

"Alright, darling," my voice was more guttural. My voice softened her and it stroked my ego. "This one first." I put my finger over the glass with the yellower liquid. "Now, don't flick it back like a shot."

"I'm not an alcoholic." She rolled her eyes.

"I never thought you were." I brought my hand to my mouth, covering a smirk.

"Why are we doing this?" She rolled her eyes. "Why did you bring me here?"

I leaned forward over the table, bringing my head down as if we were in confidence. "To know what you're made of."

"Why not ask me some questions?" Her eyes narrowed to slits, and her lips pursed, contemplating my words. "I'll tell you what you need to know."

"Darling, I could tell you the results of your last pap smear." Her eyes bugged open. I tried not to laugh. "I want to know more about you. I want you to know me. Enough, maybe, for a bit of trust."

She rested her chin in her hands, and she studied me. Really studied me. Like I was a frog being dissected.

"I know you've probably looked into me, too," I offered, as an olive branch. "You know more about me than my ex-fiancée. Now let's learn the things that you won't find from behind a computer."

"Why?" She knew exactly why. Whatever this spark was between us, I knew she felt it too.

"Because you want to." I knew that I was using *that* voice. The voice a man uses when he's seducing a woman. The kind that promised with more than words that a woman's trust would be rewarded behind closed doors.

She stayed silent, her eyes burning into me. Mistrust was written in every pore.

The challenge of it was delicious. As sweet as the drink in my hand.

I lifted my glass and nodded for her to pick up hers.

"Smell it first, then take a small taste." I brought up the liquid to my nose. The Dewars white label was not terrible for a blended scotch. It was probably what her frugal mind considered *good enough*. "When you taste it, do it slowly. Like a perfume, it'll have top, middle and bottom notes. Breathe it in. Scotch is something to be savored and loved."

Like a woman, my voice implied.

"Well, that's good to know," she swallowed to clear the lump from her throat.

I chuckled as I swirled the liquid in the glass before going through the motions of smelling it and tasting it. I did it for her benefit. For her to be able to mimic my movements, which she did. Her plump, red-painted lips delicately touched the glass, parting just the slightest bit to allow a few drops in.

Her lipstick left red marks on the glass as she set it back on the table.

"What do you think?" I felt hungry for her words. What sardonic poetry would come out of her lips?

"It tastes like scotch." She shrugged, putting the glass down without ceremony. She wanted me to fight for her reactions.

Challenge accepted.

"Now do the same with the other." I nodded to the other glass.

As I went through the motions, so did she. She didn't notice the legs of the liquid as she swirled it. She probably didn't notice that it was thicker, or that it smelled like sherry. But when it slipped past her lips and onto her tongue, I saw her brow crease. Her surprised eyes met mine.

She had noticed something. A good something, I hoped.

"What do you think?" I asked as she brought the glass down.

"It's...stronger," she conceded, but that was all the ground she would give.

I let out a small, disappointed sigh.

Geordie laughed in my earpiece. He was being a read tadger.

"You see the color?" I held my glass up to the light. "The reason it's darker than the Dewars, which is the first one we tried, is because of how the Scotch interacts with the wood."

The light danced in the tulip glass, and I caught her dark eyes following my movements. My skin heated under her scrutiny. "If a scotch is lighter, it's probably younger and sweeter. If it's darker, like this Macallan 25, then you're probably looking at something older. It's had a lot of interaction with the cask it was in. Now, if we go back to the Dewars and have a taste."

I picked up the glass of yellow liquid again and took a demonstrative sniff. She did the same as though we were synchronized in a dance. "You probably get a hint of fruit. I smell the alcohol. What about you?"

She sniffed. "Uh, same, I guess."

"Now take a sip." She did. "You probably just taste the alcohol. Maybe you'll note that it's a full body. There's no real finish to speak of."

She nodded her agreement as she put her glass down. When she looked up, there was the barest hint of a smile. I was making ground.

"Let's go back to the Macallan," I instructed, and she obeyed. That stirred something in me. Something I spent each day trying to suppress. But I couldn't think about that quite yet. Not when my pants were tenting, threatening to burst my trousers at our little cat-and-mouse game. I cleared my throat. "There's the sherry, I get the scent of Amaretto. I got a little bit of oak in there as well."

"I don't know what amaretto smells like," she admitted.

Yes! She was participating with me now. I would win her over after all.

"Amaretto is a bit like almonds."

"So... like cyanide?" Her eyebrow arched, and she looked down at her drink with renewed suspicion. This girl was good for a laugh.

"Like almonds and cherries, or fruit. Not bitter almonds like cyanide." I liked that she knew that tool of the trade. It thrilled me. She was in my line of work. Maybe not exactly the same, but she understood.

She took another taste of the Macallan without prompting. She shut her eyes and took a breath. Her tongue darted out, tasting the liquid left on her lower lip. She looked up at me through lowered lids.

That's right, darling. I thought to myself and chuckled again. *Come with me on this journey.*

"It tastes..." she spoke slowly, softly. Her voice was husky with drink. It was the most sensual thing I had heard in a long time. "Like plums. And smoke. Or caramel. It's better than the other one."

I wanted to pump my fist in the air in victory. I wanted to do a victory dance like Kylian Mbappe when he tied with Lionel Messi for the golden boot.

"That's the difference between a $20 Scotch and a thousand-dollar Scotch. It's not just the fancy label. You can taste the difference." I made my point, albeit a small one, and it was a satisfying feeling.

Her eyes bugged. She coughed, the drink going down the wrong pipe.

"How much did these drinks cost me? How much is that glass? The markup is probably insane!"

I laughed loud enough that people at nearby tables turned to look. I tried to hold it back, for the sake of discretion, but only managed a more conservative chortle.

"It cost *you* nothing. Have whatever you want. It's my treat." I leaned back, throwing an arm on the backrest of the booth.

Her eyes narrowed. "What's *that* going to cost me?"

"Nothing you don't give voluntarily." I fingered the rim of the Macallan, and smiled at her, letting a guttural moan rumble in my chest.

"You're out of your league, Callum," Geordie continued his commentary in the radio.

I wondered if her brother was speaking to her through her earpiece too, the one that she kept under the wisps of that platinum hair. What was he telling her? What was his impression of this whole encounter?

"It's just a *pleasure* for me to share this with someone." I don't know if she caught the innuendo. "You can say that scotch is my Achilles heel."

Her brow shot up. "Does that make me Penthesilea?"

"Who's that?" The name sounded vaguely familiar.

"She was a queen of the Amazons," she smirked, "and Achilles' one true love."

It was my turn to cough. It was too early in our acquaintance to be talking about one true loves.

She chuckled. "They fought on different sides of the Trojan war. They met in combat."

"Enemies to lovers, then?" I took another sip.

"Not quite," she said, and she looked down at her hands on the table, playing with the glass. "He killed her." She looked up at me through her lashes, waiting for a reaction. "Then he removed her helmet and fell in love with her beauty. I also assume that he fell in love with her character, having been well-matched in combat." She smiled, wistfully. "His ally mutilated her body and threw her into the river. At least, that's one version of it." Then her eyes drifted from her hands to mine, before she said with a note of caution, and even dread, "Is that what's going to happen now?"

I flinched.

"Gonnae gie yer mafflin a bye an day whit ye've tae day the noo ," Geordie's impatient voice came over the earpiece. *Shut your mouth and do what you're supposed to do.*

He was right. I had to stop procrastinating and do what I had to do. I just didn't want to. Yes, she was the girl who stabbed me in the neck, but in this environment, it was hard to remember that she wasn't just a beautiful woman sitting at my table.

I wondered if her own brother was in her ear, telling her to get on with it.

"Who hired you to kill Junior?" I asked.

Her brow shot up, and she smirked. "And you were doing so well, building rapport, getting some sexual tension. Now this ham-fisted segue to extract information." She tsked. "Vauxhall training has really gone downhill."

Ah, clever girl. Vauxhall wasn't on my resume. She was referring to the SIS building at Vauxhall Crossing, most famously known as the headquarters of MI-6. If she was looking for confirmation, I wouldn't be giving it to her.

"And what about you?" I turned the questions around. "Ever been to the farm?"

The farm was the colloquial name for CIA training.

"No." She laughed as if that was the most ridiculous thing in the world.

She tilted her head to the side, probably listening to something her brother was saying into her ear. She smiled again and flashed a look at me.

"Why am I here, Callum?" My name sounded sweet on her lips.

"You made a powerful enemy, darling," I told her. "The father of the man you killed... he's not taking this lying down."

She lifted her chin and removed all expression from her face. There was ice in her veins.

"Tell me what you know about Junior."

"What do you want to know?"

"You've decided to go with evasion, then?" I asked, "And I thought we were getting to know one another."

"Mr. MacLachlan..." Her voice trailed off.

"Callum," I corrected her.

"*Mister* MacLachlan," she snipped back.

"*She's got you now, lad,*" There was a chuckle in my ear from Geordie.

Her brown eyes bore into me. She was beautiful, almost frightening. If she put on dark red lipstick, a tight black dress and matched it with that intense gaze, she would be a femme fatale.

"I know you have a team," she continued, "and you are paid very well. So why the fuck does a two-man team like the Ferryman know more about your principle than you do?"

That was a good question. Why did they know more than me? It wasn't unusual for clients to lie about their personal lives. Part of our job was to research and find the true root cause of their protection issues. Sometimes we confronted them. Sometimes we didn't. But we had nothing on Junior. We couldn't even find a parking ticket.

"I don't know," I admitted. "Tell me what I'm missing."

"To what end?" She snipped. "If you choose not to believe me, then there's no point. I've already told you before."

"What evidence do you have?"

"His bank statements."

"His bank statements are behind passwords and security in a Swiss institution. There's no way you got into them."

"No way? Really?" Her brow arched, she smiled, her tone dripping with sarcasm. Then she chuckled. "Let me guess. You tried to hack into the bank itself, right?" She shook her head, almost as if she was disappointed in me. "What was the most important thing to that guy?"

"I don't know. Maybe his family." I tried to think of what priorities a man could have.

It was her turn to laugh as if that was a stupid answer.

"His family? Really?" She had an unkind smile on her lovely face. "Family might be the most important thing to you. But not to him."

"Okay, so what was most important to him?"

"He didn't have much going on upstairs," she said, her lip curling in scorn. "His passwords were easy enough if you look into his social media posts and gather what his favorite words for... women's parts are." She shrugged. "You don't have to be in MENSA to dissect that personality." Then she looked at me, challenge in her eyes. "I might not read people or their clothes well. But I can read the assholes in the room." Her eyes looked me up and down. "You are too busy seeing the best in people to see reality."

Well, that was a punch to the gut.

"Ye're fucked," Geordie said in a low mumble. "She read ye like a book."

"Yes, thank you, I don't need your commentary." I was so frustrated that I responded to Geordie out loud. Our back up was an elephant in the room. She knew I had a second with me. I knew her brother was likely somewhere nearby looking out for her.

I was tired of this act. She knew. I knew that she knew, and she knew that I knew that she knew... *Fuck it!*

"Okay, sorry," she said, with a little roll of her eyes and she flipped her hands up, palm towards me with a shrug. "Didn't mean to make you lose your cool." She looked away, through the glass into the patio. She smirked directly at Geordie. "What did he say?"

The little minx.

I cleared my throat. I heard Geordie laughing on the other end. I wanted to punch him in the face. She was down to the last sip of her scotch. I was going to lose her attention soon, and I was still nowhere near to unraveling the mysteries of the Ferryman. Though, at this point, did I care?

Whether it was just Geordie or a packed stadium, our audience was entirely too large. I wanted her alone. Truly alone. But her own brother was watching us through a camera. I didn't see him in the dining facility or the lobby. Maybe he was in the parking lot?

Geordie hadn't spotted him yet, but I knew that he was somewhere.

I had to speak to her in private. In *actual* private. Because there was something deep within me that needed to get my hands on her.

I grabbed her hand and pulled her from her seat. She didn't resist, though she could have. I tugged her to the back of the restaurant bar, down an 'Employee's Only' hallway into an office.

"We're not supposed to be back here," she said slowly as I closed the door and locked it. "I'm pretty sure they'll call the cops if they find us in here."

"They won't," I told her. She didn't look convinced. "My family owns shares in this company."

"You're an orphan."

"It's a small family."

I had my back on the closed door. She was standing in the middle of the room, eyes on me like I was a crazed animal. Maybe I was.

I stepped toward her, and she stepped back. We repeated this give and take until the back of her thighs hit the office desk. I looked down at her dress.

"Tell your brother that you don't need him right now." My fingers reached to her neckline. She tried to grab my wrists to shove me away. I tore her dress open in a single move, tiny pearls skittered loudly on the floor. The jasmine scent of her skin enveloped me, and I grew drunk on it. I saw the wires taped to her skin leading to the button cameras. I grabbed it in my hand and yanked it apart, cutting off her camera and microphone.

"Damnit! You asshole, that was a pain in the ass to assemble." She growled. The woman actually growled. I'd never heard a woman do that before. I liked it.

"I'll replace it. Give me ten, Geordie," I said, before reaching into my pocket to turn off my own comms but hesitated to add, "Actually, make that fifteen."

He was still snickering when I clicked off the radio.

She looked at me, confusion coloring her face. She was mad. But she wasn't saying no. With her dress hanging open, I gazed at her exposed breasts and taut, brown nipples. A beautiful, lean line ran down the center of her abs and I salivated at the thought of running my tongue along those gorgeous valleys. She was irresistible.

It wasn't what I normally liked. I had always thought that I preferred a slim figure. Tall, slim, elegant. But there was something about the sheer power of this woman, and how the muscles flexed under her skin. I wanted to pull down her dress even further to see more of that tanned flesh. I wanted to get my teeth on her, to mark her and bruise her beautiful skin.

I put my hand on either side of her waist, opening the dress even further. She was warm. Her skin was smooth. She was tan all over, but the places that would normally be covered by clothes were much lighter. There was a distinct line of paler skin that started at her breasts. She wasn't the kind of woman to put on an unnatural tan or bronzed in the nude. Her lines were natural, a gift from the sun. No, this coloring was what God had intended and it unlocked a fetish I didn't know I had.

She tilted her head down at where my hands touched her skin, then, without moving her face, looked up at me. That look telegraphed *Where are you going with this?*

I leaned in to kiss her. She was short, and it was a bit of work. But it was worth it, because the scent of her jasmine perfume wafted around me, and her lips tasted like caramel.

At first, she didn't move and didn't return the kiss. She kept her lips firmly closed. Then she climbed onto her tiptoes, giving her a little height to meet me. Her lips relaxed just a fraction, and I took the chance to invade her mouth with my tongue.

Her gasp was an unexpected song that heated my blood. Her hands flew around my neck. Her nails dug into my skin through my suit. When she released a small, low, throaty moan I pulled away. If I stayed any longer, I'd push her against the wall and take her right there.

"Mo Leannan." I growled, taking a calming breath.

I lunged back in again. Our tongues and teeth clashed and my hand on her waist snaked around until I was pulling her into me. Her hands fisted on the lapels of my blazer, pulling me closer. Her moans and her breath were in tandem with mine. She wanted this as much as I did, and that made me rock hard.

She pulled away first. Her fists flattening and pushing me away. But even that was a victory for me. She blinked first in our game of chicken.

"What does that mean?" she panted.

"What does what mean?"

"That language. Whatever you just said before you...you..."

"Before I kissed you the second time?" I supplied, "It's Scots."

"Isn't that Gaelic?" Her nose crinkled.

"We'll correct your misconceptions some other time, *Brèagha*. We'll have time to get to know each other, aye?" I was throbbing and thinking about her in my home as I explored that tight little body. I'd moan these Scottish words of endearment to her until she knew them as well as I did, and maybe she'd use some of her own words for me.

But for that to happen, I needed her to listen to me. I needed her to cooperate with me before Rashid found out who she was and sent other people after her.

"I meant what I said. I am not the only person sent to find you. Just the first one here." I cleared my throat. "Lay low. Not because I tell you to, but to protect yourself. To protect your family."

"I don't take orders well."

"Clearly." I couldn't help a chuckle.

"Why should I trust you?" She asked, her breathing still as heavy and shallow as mine. "What do I get out of this? What do you?"

"Whatever you want." That was as much truth as I was comfortable with. She could have anything she wanted from me because I needed her. Now that I had tasted her, I couldn't imagine a world without those lips.

I leaned in, putting my nose to the place beneath her ear and drifted down to her throat, smelling that jasmine perfume again.

"Do you wear that scent all over your body, or just right here?" I had to know.

"Wouldn't you like to know, you pervert." She playfully punched my shoulder. I rubbed the spot as if it hurt.

It was a herculean effort to step away from her. My time with her was coming to an end. Leo or Geordie would be storming in at any moment, and I needed to tell her what I wanted from her right now, before the opportunity passed.

"I mean it, Atalanta," I whispered into her ear. "Lay low. Wait until you hear from me."

CHAPTER SIXTEEN

"Lay low. Wait until you hear from me." He was one part pleading, one part demanding.

Who the fuck does he think he is?

At least he had the decency to look as disheveled and out of breath as I did. I think he read the defiance in my mind because he let out a low, rumbling groan of frustration. Through clenched teeth he said, "I'm trying to protect you. Just do what you're told."

"Oh, aye Laird Callum. Right away Laird Callum!" I hoped that my sarcasm was as thick and heavy as the whiskey that was still on his tongue. "Why should I listen? Why would you protect me? Who am I to you? And why do you think you can defend me better than I can defend myself?"

"I don't know yet... *Fuck!*" I liked how he said the word fuck. It was masculine and promised passion and violence. He used his perfect British voice, but when he said the word "fuck", it was pure Scottish. It was the hottest thing I had ever heard. "You don't deserve to have the crosshairs put on you if Junior is everything you say. But you cannot fathom the kind of wealth you are up against. Rashid Khan is a good man, but he has enough wealth to destroy the world and you've ripped out a piece of his soul. Give me time to fix this."

"You seem to think that you can fix impossible situations."

"There aren't many problems I can't make right," he continued, his voice crooning in my ear, sending goosebumps down my spine, "Tell me who hired you."

"That's classified, *Laird* Callum." Why was my voice so breathy? It shouldn't be so breathy. Come on diaphragm, do your fucking job.

"I'll find out anyway." He glared down at me.

"And why would I care?"

"Whoever hired you probably did it so that Rashid Khan would give every-thing his son would have inherited to another relative." He was gritting his teeth. His fingers on my waist tightened. A little more pressure, and he might leave marks. "A relative who will donate that to the KNF. You get that those are bad guys, right?"

"It would have been no better in Junior's hands. One rich man is as corrupt as the next."

"You don't care who hired you? You don't care what those people are capable of or what they want to do?"

"No," I told him. His shock made me smile. "If someone hired me to kill the last person who commissioned my services, I'd do it. Anyone who hires an assassin is up to some evil shit. No one pays this kind of money to kill good guys."

"You bite the hand that feeds you?"

"I'll bite whoever I want. Even the hand that pays me blood money. The people I kill and the people who hire me are *all* bad guys. I'm a bad guy, too. No one who can afford my prices ever got their wealth by honest means. Frankly, no one that rich made it by being decent."

"You hate the rich?" he snorted, bordering on offended.

I sneered. "I eat the rich."

I pushed him again, and he relented, taking a step away from me. I look down at my dress. The front was wide open down to the waist, the wires we had been placed so carefully dangled limply by what was left of the tape.

"Fuck," I whispered as I tried to salvage it. But there was nothing to salvaged. I was about to yell at him, but he was staring at me and smiling. I tried to hold my dress together. "You can look away now, asshole."

He didn't look away. He didn't stop grinning.

I ran my fingers through my hair to make sure that was still presentable. Without a mirror, there wasn't any real way to verify it. As I turned to go to the door, I heard a rustling sound from him. Then he grabbed my elbow, and I felt a heavy, wool jacket fall on my shoulders. He brought the front of it tight together, overlapping them like a robe and covering my exposed breasts. He brought his other hand to my face so that I had to look up at him, tilting my jaw up until it craned my neck.

I fucking hate tall people.

"I mean it, Lea." My name on his lips, the way it lilted and danced on his low voice. It was unsettling. Arousing? No, unsettling. It was unsettling. "Lay low. Stay safe. Promise me."

I stared up at his eyes. They were green. Or hazel. Both? I had nothing but matte brown eyes, flat, and constant, without a fleck or hint of any other color.

"Laird Callum..." I glanced at the blazer he put around me. He was standing in nothing but his silk shirt and I could see every curve and muscle of his body. "*If* I lay low, it will be because I corroborate your information and choose to do so. Not because you told me to." I wanted it to come out biting, and sarcastic, but it came out warm. Weak.

He grinned again. I wanted to punch that expression right off his face, but at this proximity, I was at a bad angle.

A palm strike to his chin would be really satisfying right now.

"I'll be coming back for another taste, *darling.*" That word again. He leaned down and brought his lips near my ear and in a whisper, he said, "I'll replace your wire and your dress. Keep the blazer. It looks good on you."

"Why? So, people can think that we fucked back here?"

"They're already going to think that we fucked," he said going back to his full height, his finger tracing the line of my jaw. "Why? Do you want to? I can talk Geordie into giving us another thirty minutes."

"Please. I felt that thing. It won't take you more than thirty seconds." Again, I wanted to sound mean, but I couldn't keep the little whimper from my voice. What was he doing to me?

"Don't challenge me," he growled. It was low and rumbled deep in his chest. I could feel it vibrating through his whole body. "Get out of here. Now."

"Or what?" What was it with him and always trying to tell me what to do? I tried to stand up straighter, but there was nothing that would ever change our height difference. He made me feel small and delicate.

"Or you're going to need a bloody safe word," his voice was coiled with tension. His one hand was clenched into a fist, and the one on my cheek started to tremble. He was vibrating with his restraint.

I liked it. I liked the effect I had on him. I felt powerful and wicked.

I leaned into him. I came up on my tiptoes and brought my lips to his ear and whispered, "It's Gemini."

He let out a guttural moan. I pulled away, held his blazer closed around my bare torso, turned, and unlocked the door. I flung it open to escape. I won this round. He was going to suffer blue balls.

In the hallway was a brunette man, about Callum's height, with his hands in fists by his side. He looked across the way at my brother who stood with his teeth bared, ready to strike. I had no idea how long they had been there. Both of them turned to look at me, then at Callum. The stranger's eyebrow rose, and a corner of his mouth lifted.

"*What's this*?" Leo asked in Tagalog, shock written all over his face.

"*Wala.*" I lifted my head and strode out the door. *Nothing.*

I practically stomped my way down the hall and just before I had gotten to the main dining room, I heard that deep voice call out, "Stay away from that Brett guy! Or he will end up disappearing."

"Is that a fucking promise?" I yelled back.

The two men chuckled as Leo and I walked away without a backward glance.

CHAPTER SEVENTEEN

Leo had barely slammed the door of the car when he asked, "What happened?"

"We'll talk about it later."

"What happened to your dress?"

"We'll talk about it *later*!"

He started the car and we drove away in silence.

I was glad that twin telepathy wasn't real. Leo didn't need to know that I was still stuck on that kiss. That I felt Callum's cock against my belly as he pulled me to my toes. He didn't need to know that I kissed him back and longed to tear his shirt open and claw at his flesh.

What did he want? What could the former fiancé of supermodel Pippa Fox want from me? Was he helping me because his dick reacted to me? Was that it?

That would be incredibly disappointing. Almost... hurtful.

It took us thirty minutes to drive home. That was the magic number anywhere in Los Angeles County. Almost any commute was thirty minutes, give or take. It doesn't matter if you were traveling five or fifty miles. It was just a part of the LA magic.

Once we were at our driveway, I was ready to talk. I spilled that Rashid Khan Senior had a hit out on whoever killed his son. That others were likely on their way. Then I said that Callum wanted me to lay low.

Leo nodded at that information, never interrupting. My hands were shaking by the end of my tale. I had never been in the crosshairs. People were in mine. I was the aggressor. Never on defense. I didn't like this feeling much and I wanted my equilibrium back.

"Did he..." my brother cleared his throat. "Did he try anything with you? Anything that you didn't want?" Leo swallowed and shut his eyes before opening them again. "Do I need to handle him?"

I turned to him, my face blank and I played dumb. "What do you mean?"

"You know what I mean."

"If he did, do you think I would have let him live?"

"I don't fucking know, do I Lea?" Leo punched the steering wheel. "The feed was cut. When I went to get you, his hulking friend was outside telling me to give you guys another eight minutes. I nearly gutted him in the hallway. I absolutely would have if you hadn't come out of the room when you did."

He took several deep breaths. I unconsciously matched his breathing. It was something that we had done since we were babies. Or maybe even earlier than that.

"But he's right," he tilted his head backwards and stared at the car's ceiling. "It might not be such a bad idea for you to lay low. Did he seem sincere?"

Yes. His eyes, his hands, his mouth were so earnest and honest that I wanted to drown in them. He promised me pleasure and satisfaction and I wanted to know more.

I shook my head. That wasn't going to work at all. "I have to go to Kemet."

"I'll take it."

"It's not a mission for you." He had made it clear over a year ago that he wouldn't return to Kemet or the Bass Medical camps. He never told me what happened, but I had a strong suspicion that it had something to do with a woman.

"I can handle it!" He was mad. I wasn't used to him being mad. "I want you to lay low. Just like he said."

I didn't like that my brother agreed with Callum. I didn't like it one bit. They weren't ganging up on me, but I felt outnumbered. A decision was getting pushed down on me.

I knew that I was losing this mission. I didn't hate that. I hated that Leo would have to do it for me.

But the decision was made. It was decided without words. There was only one thing left for me to say.

"So," I started. "Have you eaten?"

CHAPTER EIGHTEEN

Geordie and I watched them walk away, their identical gaits heading out those heavy wooden doors and out of the hotel.

"Fifteen minutes, huh?" Geordie said with a chuckle. "Did you get what you needed done?" When they were out of sight, he turned towards me. "Did you bang her?"

I snorted. "No."

But we could have. Her soft voice telling me "It's Gemini" would haunt my dreams and spring my cock to life.

She molded to my body as though we had been long time lovers. She responded with bravado and had given me a fucking safe word. She had to have known what that would do to my head.

Geordie and I left the bar and went up to the 50th floor, to the penthouse that was reserved for only the most discerning of patrons and prominent shareholders. I was both.

It was a three bedroom, three bath apartment with its own private elevator. The living room windows overlooked the massive city of Los Angeles, from the city all the way to the distant hills, bisected by ribbons of highway.

I stood in front of the large pane and watched the soft lights of the living room cast my reflection back at me.

This was her city. The city that she lived in since she was a toddler.

I wanted to put a tracker in her jacket. Or in her hair. Or in her skin. Maybe in her teeth? I wanted to track her every movement, and make sure that she did stand down for her own safety. I wanted to *make* her safe. It was a protectiveness that I hadn't felt for a woman before.

But I didn't. I didn't want to violate her privacy... yet. But my resolve to be the good guy in all of this was slowly waning the more stubborn she became.

Geordie stood by me, offering me a tumbler of Scotch. It was the Macallan 25, something I always kept in stock. The scent would normally bring me peace, but Lea's jasmine perfume was slowly over taking it as the fragrance I'd obsess over.

"What's going on with you, Callum?" Geordie asked.

"I don't know."

"I don't see it," Geordie sighed, "She looks wee. Women should be a little more...well... *more*. She's sure got a smart mouth though, so I can see that appeal."

I nodded in agreement, though Geordie's disparaging remarks hit me in the gut. She was wee. But she was a real woman with a voice she wasn't afraid to use and a body that was as powerful as her sarcasm.

"Is she worth losing Rashid as a client?" Geordie wasn't letting up. "She'd better be worth it."

"I can't kill her," I said, plainly. "And I'm not a gun for hire."

"Yes, but she is. And she's off her rocker." The thought of that made me smile. Geordie continued, "Jesus, man. She's just your type then."

"She hates rich people."

"So she obviously hates you, then."

"Aye, but I'm no Baas or Khan," I protested.

"You've seen their house? That's what being normal is. You're a millionaire saying you're normal compared to billionaires... That makes you even more out of touch."

"Aye, maybe I am." All the while we spoke, I had been sipping my glass and it was now empty. I refilled it again, feeling the slight buzz coming on. "But she's not exactly panhandling."

We stood in silence, staring at the moving lights again. Los Angeles was unlike any other city in the world. It wasn't cramped or ornate like the old European capitals. Los Angeles lacked the long, intricate history of European cities.

Instead of the grime of a past, it got the glitz, glamor and sunshine of a future.

The bright lights drowned out the stars. I missed the stars reflecting on the loch and how the moon's reflection would dance on the ripples of the cold water. I missed my country house, and the stone walls. I'd take that over glass and concrete any day.

"Is it only because she sent an SOS on the radio after she stabbed you in the neck?" Geordie said the last phrase with emphasis.

"At first, it was. Aye," I admitted. "Another assassin would have killed me. But there's something else happening. Something with Müller, and Junior, and all of it... If I manage to save her too, then all the better. It'd square things up between us."

"So you can feck her, then?"

"No, you gobshite." I wanted to smack the back of his head for talking about her that way.

Geordie chuckled.

"I finally went through everything on Müller's phone from Argentina." He paused for dramatic effect. "He was texting Junior's location to an unknown number. Presumably the Ferryman. I'm going through more. I have his bank passwords and I have to go through things line by line. But we have our mole, if not the guy who ordered the hit. I just can't find a reason why yet."

That was good. I could push the blame for Rashid's son from Lea and place it on Müller.

Geordie went to bed after he finished his drink.

I didn't sleep that night. I simply looked out at lights that were Los Angeles County. It went on forever into the surrounding hills that were always brown from the perpetual droughts and brush fires. Nothing like my cold, wet, Scotland. I wonder how a girl like Lea would fare in that kind of climate. I could imagine her on a leather chair, covered in fur blankets by a roaring, open fire as the snow fell outside in the huge farmland I lived on.

Does that make me Penthesilea?

What an obscure reference. It was a side note in Homer's *Iliad* that it rarely got referenced. But she knew it. I had forgotten that name until she reminded me of it. Was it fate that her name was tacked to the end of Pentehesilea's? Was it written in the stars? Was I the Achilles that would love her and kill her, and my allies would destroy her?

I was exhausted. I rested my eyes.

But her face flashed through my mind. Her face, red and torn in my hands, her small eyes shut, and blood trickling down her silver hair onto hot sand. I heard my own distant voice crying her name. It was just a flash. A moment.

It jolted me on the armchair where I had fallen asleep, a glass still clutched in my fingers.

"That won't happen," I said, my hand tightening on the glass. "I will make it so."

The wheels were turning in my mind. I could get her out of the crosshairs. I could fix this.

As the sky changed from black to a dark blue, the city's lights flickered off. The sun crested over the eastern jagged mountains. With my phone in my hand, I waited. And waited.

When the phone vibrated, I almost jumped.

The notification from the secure video app announced the incoming call.

I took a deep breath and accepted the call.

Rashid's face popped up on one screen. In a smaller window was Müller. His face was as cool and impersonal as alpine ice.

"Callum." Rashid greeted from his London office. I could see the Thames behind him. "I want updates."

"I think I'm closing in," I said, flat, trying to give away nothing.

"I have new information," Müller interjected. "I have traced the scalpel used on MacLachlan." The typically expressionless face soured into a smile. He was the cat with the bloody, dying canary in his mouth.

I kept my face cool. Indifferent. Unfeeling.

"How did you come by this information?" I asked slowly.

"I called Mr. Alexander Baas. His medical company made the scalpel, and he traces them with a microscopic serial number. I thought that your man, Mr. George Campbell, was going to investigate it, but I suppose that with your injuries, it became less of a priority." He looked at me through his screen, his left eye twitching, watching me for signs of deception.

"Mm," I grunted. Everything about Müller, his cold eyes, his placid indifference, made me smell a trap. "We have not had a chance to follow up yet."

I prayed that Alexander had not given anything away.

"Good," Rashid said, his voice low, even and quiet. It was menacing to see the man this way. The benevolent, friendly man turned into a villain. "Follow the trail Müller. Update Callum when you can."

"Might I make another suggestion." Time to lay out my cards and hope that he took the bait. "The assassin is, of course, responsible. But wouldn't it be better to bring you the man who ordered the hit? Especially since this was the second attempt. We can assume that the first hit was put out by the same person. As I understand, we are still unsure of who that was." Rashid leaned in closer to his camera. "What if I brought you that man?"

Müller's eyes narrowed. It was so slight that I almost missed it.

I took a breath and tried to make my blood cold. I wanted my delivery to be as frigid and expressionless as it could be. "An assassin is a gun. I'm more interested in the hand that fired it."

Rashid stared into his camera, and it was as if he was sitting across the table from me now. As though we were in a staring contest. I had to close this deal now.

"Think about it, Rashid." I softened my voice. "You'll get your revenge, but it will be pointed at the person who was ultimately responsible. I can bring you that man." Or woman, I suppose, but it wasn't the right time for gender equality.

Rashid Khan leaned back. I knew the man well enough to know that he was contemplating his next words. He rapped his nails on the desk, one finger at a time from pinky to index finger. The rhythm was like an executioner's drum.

"A hundred million dollars to whoever gets the person responsible for the death of my son."

Rashid cut the call. It was over. He agreed, somewhat. That was as good as could have been expected. Now, I just needed Lea to tell me who hired her. I may even be able to get that information from Leo. Surely, he'd do anything to protect his sister. I was willing to try anything at this point.

I sat there for as long as I could before I started to feel the sweat and strain from the restless night. I went into my room to take a cold shower.

I could still hear her voice in my ear.

Who am I to you? she had asked. I didn't know.

But I very badly wanted to find out.

CHAPTER NINETEEN

Mojave Desert, California, USA

I stared up at the stars. I was lying on the manhole at the entrance of our bunker. There was nothing quite like the crisp, dry desert night. In the Mojave, there was no light pollution to dampen the inky, blank night and the stars appeared the way they did a thousand years ago, before electricity and engines polluted the sky.

I got to participate in my most meditative hobby, staring at the sky and thinking about Greek mythology. Of course, there were the stories of each astrological sign. Aries, the ram with the golden fleece from the stories about Jason. Taurus, the minotaur in the labyrinth. Cancer, the crab that squeezed Hercules' toe and was kicked into the sky and got stuck there forever. Then there was the Scorpion, at Orion's heel, locked in an eternal battle. There was also the thirteenth zodiac, Ophiuchus, the snake charmer.

There was a Greek myth for everything, and many of them lived in the sky.

My fascination first started when I discovered the story of the twins. Most people only know them as Gemini, the constellation for those born at the beginning of the summer. Not many people know their individual names – Castor and Pollux.

They were born identical, and indistinguishable by looks or manners. But one was a son of a mortal King, the other the son of Zeus. The immortal Pollux was the fastest, the smartest, and the strongest demi-God. He survived the Trojan war. The mortal brother, Castor, did not.

Mourning the loss of his brother, Pollux begged his father Zeus to resurrect him. His wish was granted, but at the price that the twins would spend half their time in the mortal world and half of it in the stars.

I knew which twin I was. It played out day after day in our life. I would fall, and Leo would pick me up.

My twin. My brother. The good one.

I wondered, sometimes, if Castor in the sky ever looked at his twin and felt like a burden. Did he ever wish to cross the river Styx and unburden his brother? Did Pollux ever wish that he didn't have to spend his life carting his lesser brother around? Did he ever want to live his own life? If so, did he keep that a secret? In their eternity in the sky, would Pollux ever tell his feelings to Castor? Did either of them fall in love and sever their bonds to start new families?

When I couldn't entertain the uncertainty anymore, I looked up at Gemini one more time and made a wish – a wish for Leo to be safe.

I got up off the dry, dusty ground, climbed into the manhole and entered the bunker.

The screens in the control room were lit up, each screen on a different news channel with bobbing heads narrating current events at a low volume. I turned up the sound on Callisandra because she was the least annoying. Maybe it was because her male counterparts were too slick-haired, with their orange tans. Callisandra had bags under her eyes and flaws on her skin. She was weather worn and gaunt, and real, but beautiful for it.

"Alexander Baas, billionaire and CEO of Bass Medical Technology responds to criticism that his employees are not adequately protected when working in conflict zones." She said in an authoritative tone.

Her screen turned into an image of the brown-haired Alexander Baas, square jawed and amicable, speaking kindly into a microphone thrust into his face. "I want all my employees to be safe, which is why they get training in survival and evacuation." His charming voice made him sound like a Hollywood actor. "It takes a lot of courage to work in some of these areas, and if they want to leave at any point, they can do so without any kind of negative consequences from the company. We always try to help them find different positions if it gets too troublesome for them in these, admittedly, very dangerous, ungoverned spaces."

I met him once. It was only a couple years ago, but it felt like a different lifetime.

Kemet was a semi-autonomous zone in the sense that it was a complete no man's land. It was autonomous from its lack of government and minimal regulations.

It was a high desert country with frigid evenings and hot, windy days. It was a long and narrow unwanted patch of land, and recent conflicts in the Middle East thrust refugees into its uninhabitable spaces. Temporary tent cities were starting to become permanent hut-villes.

To one side, they had the Kemet National Front, or the KNF. On the other was the Kemet People's Liberation Army or KPLA. Each side would plow over the small strip of land until the international community came in, planted the blue flag of the United Nations and declared it a protected zone. Then the charities came in, and money poured in as pop singers and actors were invited to the camps to raise awareness.

But there was no escape for its residents no matter how many concerts and how many banquets were held in their honor. So, they built schools. Communal farms were started and some form of stability and regulations helped alleviate the dangers in the ungoverned space. A market was formed.

As though things weren't bad enough for the people already, the greatest misfortune happened. They discovered oil under their feet.

The protections put in place were threatened by politicians, the refugees were vilified for living on charity and the poor, barefoot kids were called parasites and their parents were criticized for procreating. Of course, there were no exceptions for women who were raped, or for parents who died in the conflict. It was all written off as a problem with "those" people. Victims became villains, and the aid stopped coming.

That was when Baas Medical and its CEO came in on a white horse, ready to save the day. He came with aid, finances, and an ever-rotating group of doctors and teachers.

I rarely enjoyed my life as a nurse. In fact, I usually despised it. But in Kemet, there was a sense of urgency in the air, like the world was wrong and it was everyone's duty to try to inject a little justice, a little fairness and a little mercy into everything. Or maybe it was the culture of the Baas Refugee Camps.

The brochures, the walls, the logos all had the paraphrased Ghandi quote: *"be the change you wish to see in the world."*

Alexander Baas spent his adult life combating suffering. The doctors and nurses his company sent out to Kemet were always briefed about fairness, mercy and cultural awareness from the moment they accepted the contract, until they were released into the field. And everyone seemed to truly believe in that mission. I did too and that's why I went to Kemet.

At the start, there were weekly meetings that he attended personally. Doctors complained about addicts trying to steal what little medical grade narcotics they had on hand. I saw nurses complain of fathers who beat their wives, and mothers who neglected their children. There was stealing, violence, and the constant threat of communicable diseases running rampant through the overcrowded camps.

A doctor had his face in his hands. He was frustrated with corruption and crime. He was frustrated with the sheer inhumanity that occurred in the human misery that surrounded us.

Alexander, in his loose-fitting tan shirt and cargo pants listening with rapt attention and sympathy. He nodded at the right places, looked concerned when he needed to, and brought a hand to his chin when he was contemplating something.

Then, with a gentle tilt of his head, he smiled, and his eyes glazed and seemed distant. He looked down at the blue faced Rolex on his wrist and fidgeted with it a moment before he spoke.

"I understand your frustrations." Then that crisp, deep voice, full of authority and sophistication swept over us, and it felt like it crawled over my skin and into my mind like hypnosis. "We are doing a thankless job. With more pain than anyone should ever have to endure, and we will never get as much as we give. But I see what you are doing. Isn't one life saved worth all the heartache? Isn't one morsel of good in this wasteland, one moment of justice, and a crumb of mercy worth a little of our suffering?"

He went on and on about loving humanity, and all its intricacies, its lights, and its darks, the pure as well as the gray. Then he raised his hand, palms out. "Thank you to all of you, for your time, your patience, your dedication to serving humanity."

He took the time to look each person in the eye, one by one.

When he spoke, my burdens were lifted from my shoulders and were replaced with this conviction to do good and be good. He was that rare human specimen that deserved to be called a leader.

I dragged Leo in. If we were going to be nurses, then we could at least do good. We continued to rotate in and out of Baas camps. It was the most honest money that we ever made. We used to travel there together, as a sort of brother-sister bonding vacation, but with the benefit of clearing some of Leo's conscience.

It was a humid, frigid day in the nurse's tent when a beautiful, dark-skinned doctor with wild, ringlet curls bouncing with her movements entered. She was looking impatiently at her watch. She scanned us one by one, as we lounged in make-shift chairs and ate power bars, awaiting our assignments. Her eyes fell on me and my brother. Her head tilted. Then she pointed a finger at Leo.

"Come with me," she said in a crisp French accent.

Her name, I would later find out, was Dr. Chloe Laurent. She specialized in women and children's health, and she recruited Leo to be her assistant.

"Why you?" I asked Leo.

"She said I looked like I could be good with kids, and that the women wouldn't be scared of me."

"I'm a woman."

"So?"

"If she needed someone to work with women and kids, shouldn't she have picked me, because *I'm a woman*?"

"I don't know, Lea. I'm not going to ask."

"Why not?"

"Because I like working with the kids."

I didn't know that Leo was good with children until I saw it with my own eyes. On that trip, he spent time in the open fields with a soccer ball, tumbling with the children. When the weather prevented that, he did crafts in one of the large school tents, pretending not to know Arabic and using one or two words to communicate. He was fluent, of course, but his cover as a nurse relied on him being amiable, and unremarkable.

He delighted in showing the kids the one or two Arabic words he "learned," and they'd giggle at his butchered pronunciation. The kids, in turn, tried to speak English to him. He took a shining to a little orphan, Asa, who became his little shadow.

It was a shock to me when, after a year, he decided he was never going back.

I didn't question. I didn't ask. His expression told me that he didn't want to talk about it. He was upset. I made him some Arroz Caldo and left him alone.

Leo going back to Kemet was a big deal.

It was my mission. My mission that he now had to take over because of my fuck up. As Pollux would bail out Castor, Leo would bail me out as well.

He'd hate this mission.

He'd hate what we were about to do to Kemet. We were going to throw it into complete and utter chaos. For a good cause, of course. The person we were taking out wasn't called the Butcher because he was good at cutting ribeyes. But killing bad men didn't always bring a happy ending. The worst things in the world weren't wars. They were power vacuums. The only ray of hope was if whoever gained dominance was marginally better than the one that was taken out.

There were no guarantees in life, and the only thing I could do – the only thing any of us could do – was wait and wait for hell to rain down on our heads.

There was a Greek myth for this feeling as well.

Damocles was a courtier who went up to a king and envied him for his wealth and opulence. The King gave him a chance to sit on his throne. As Damocles enjoyed the rich food and basked in the attention of the kowtowing servants, he looked up to see that above his head was a sword, attached by the thinnest string.

The food turned to ash in his mouth and the joy in his new wealth disappeared, replaced by fear, waiting for this sword to fall on his skull.

That's how this felt. I envied the greatness and wealth that came with our job. I wanted to be the greatest, a self-proclaimed demigod Kharon. Now there was a sword that hung over my head, waiting for the slightest breeze to slice into my skull. It would happen. I knew that I would go like Tito Leo, one day. Violently, and execution style.

I knew it the moment I made my first kill. That was why I didn't want to bring Leo into this, but he gave me no choice.

CHAPTER TWENTY

Los Angeles, California, USA

I looked out at Los Angeles. Being this high up gave the impression of being a God; distant, and in control of everyone below. A man could get used to that feeling.

I held the phone in front of my face as I rang up one of the world's real-life demigods.

"Alex!" I greeted the face as it popped up on my phone. "Is this a bad time?"

The man was in a button-down shirt, a leather bomber jacket, and a pair of black aviators. He looked like Gregory Peck. He had that old school Hollywood look now. Geordie thought he had surgical help to achieve that effect. I think that he just grew into his features.

I could hear the *whomp-whomp-whomp* of helicopter propellers in the distance.

"No, it's always a good time, Callum. How are you? Geordie said you had a mishap!"

My school friend was a far cry from the scrawny, tawny haired teen with Coke bottle glasses wearing the striped, blue necktie of our alma mater. From kindergarten to A-levels, we had been thrust into one another's circle. While I started Caledonia Security, a modest venture grossing a comfortable profit, Alex created a medical empire and was known for his Midas touch. He found new ways to innovate solutions to the ever changing, ever evolving infections and crises around the globe. Further, he was a philanthropist, giving millions to charity every year.

He was the unlikely hero that the world needed, and I was exceedingly proud of his transformation.

"There was no permanent harm," I told him, rotating my arm in its socket to emphasize my point.

"I already gave Geordie everything I could find. Is there more I can help with?"

"Yes. Did you get a call from a man by the name of Dieter Müller?"

He coughed, clearing his throat as the wind picked up around him. The propellers got louder, and the wind kicked up the dust around him, his hair blowing around his face.

"Where are you?" I shouted into the phone.

Alex brought the lapel of his jacket in front of his face to block out the dust. "I just finished a class. I'm learning how to fly helicopters!"

I laughed. The man collected hobbies like penguins collected stones. By the end of the fiscal year, he would have his own helicopter and be ready to innovate that mode of transportation, I had no doubt.

The wind started to die down as the offending helicopter flew away. Alex turned back to his camera.

"Yes! He said he worked with you." He looked concerned, his brows disappearing behind his mirrored glasses. "I gave him as little information as I could. I imagine that if he was working with you, then you would be the one calling me. Not him."

"That's right," I exhaled in relief.

Alexander was no fool. He had always been sharp as a whip.

"I told him that it was linked to medical supplies sent to Rashid Khan's Argentinian NGO." He ran a hand through his hair. "I'm sorry. Should I have said something different? I wasn't sure."

I smiled. "No, old friend. You did just fine. I wanted to call and just make sure I had the whole picture."

"Of course but..." as he assumed a light canter, the airfield coming into view behind him. "I had some of my people investigate this Müller chap. It's not good news I'm afraid."

"What did you find?"

"Well, I was tipped off when we couldn't find any information on him at all. That's always a bit suspicious. His records were non-existent. It turns out that his name is not Müller at all. That name came out of the French Foreign Legion with a French citizenship."

"When?"

"Well, before 2010, of course. The French no longer give citizenships to those whose real names have serious crimes attached to them."

"But they used to." I said it as a statement, but Alex took it as a question.

"It's complicated, but yes. A man could join the French Foreign legion under a falsified name and change their identity and get a French citizenship at the end of their service."

"Is that what Müller did?"

"I have it under good authority that he got in under the name Isa De la Croix, but that was also a fake name." I was unsure what was obvious about that, but I didn't respond and let him continue. "I don't have any contacts that could give me any more than that, though. None of my people were close to him, and those legionnaires are an impenetrable wall. I thought maybe your man could look into it further for you."

I heard the click of a car unlocking, and the next thing I knew, he was getting into his one-of-a-kind, made-just-for-him white electric car.

"I'll send what information I have to you," he said, pressing a button and putting his phone on a holder. The car engine probably turned on, but there was no sound.

"Thank you for that information."

"Of course. The blood of chocolatiers and all that nonsense…"

When I got off the phone, I considered this new information. Alexander had never led me astray before. He was the kind of man who always wanted to be of service to everyone. But he kept his sources close to the vest. He was especially good to the St. Michael's network. He had gone to bat for me when I started my security company, sending investors my way until I had more than I knew what to do with!

Speaking of chocolatiers, Geordie entered the room with his laptop.

"I have more information for you." He slapped the laptop in front of me on the table. "Junior was dirty. It was like your girl said. I got into his accounts using his passwords. His favorite derogative for a woman and their parts was *Hairy Minge.* A few swapped out letters for special characters and I got in."

"Good lord, he really was a bastard."

"They always are, aren't they?" Geordie clicked a few things, and a spreadsheet came up. "Look at these incoming transactions." His finger hovered over the screen over several large deposits. "All from the same account. It's from an account based in the Cayman Islands. After some digging it's associated with the triangle trade."

"Shit." I wiped the sleep and frustration from my face. "People, guns, or drugs?"

"People and drugs," Geordie confirmed. "Your girl was on to something."

She wasn't my girl. She was a woman and belonged to no one. Not yet.

Geordie elaborated on the transactions, the finances and deposits each time he went to two specific countries–one in Argentina, and another in Amsterdam. Those were the places that he had favorite brothels, or so he had led us to believe.

"He probably met his contacts at those visits. It would make sense, but it's hard to get confirmation unless we do a full investigation, and I don't know if it'd be worth it at this point."

"So, he wasn't there as just a tourist."

"It could have been both."

I brought in Geordie, and we called Hugo Martin, our French Legionnaire, and told him what Alex had just told me.

"Can you find Dieter Müller's real name?"

"How old is he?" Hugo asked.

"About 47, maybe 48? I'll send what we have."

"Bon." *Good.* Then Hugo hung up.

Geordie said dryly. "He's got a real way with words."

CHAPTER TWENTY-ONE

Mojave Desert, California, USA

When the name Rafiq Abadi, head honcho for the KPLA in Kemet, crossed my desk, I thought about declining the job. The payout was enormous. The buyer, who was recommended by the man who hired me to kill Ivan Leclerc, made great arguments for why Abadi, nicknamed the Butcher, needed to die.

And he supplied pictures.

Women were mutilated and raped. Boys conscripted to be child-soldiers. There were a dozen girls that he married far too young and forced them to bear children when they, themselves, should have been going to school. And corpses. Rows and rows of corpses mounted high on spikes to strike fear into those who would defy him. Then, there were also the videos of prisoners beheaded by a dull knife, the Butcher's boot on the man's temple as he cut the delicate flesh of his throat.

He was medieval in his idea of leadership, and he was far too comfortable with gore and violence. He was the embodiment of evil.

He had been the target of no less than four drone strikes. They didn't so much as singe him.

Best case, the man died, and another idiot took his place. We got paid and the world kept on turning.

Worst case? There was a power vacuum with the KPLA. Conflicts within the group would arise. The KNF would take advantage of the chaos and try to gain control of the territory and the oil.

Refugees would be killed in the crossfire, and we couldn't predict if that would be worse than the number of casualties that were lost every day to the skirmishes that happened around the camp.

But it was still better than letting him live and continue his reign of terror.

One, or both, of the organizations, the KNF and KPLA, would sweep through at some point. They'd decimate these camps to control the oil unless the international community sent soldiers and tanks. But they wouldn't. Not for some unknown refugees who couldn't vote or contribute to political campaigns. Kemet was like a bubble floating on the breeze. A change in the wind or the slightest touch would make it just disappear. It was only a matter of time.

I should have known that when I made that decision, my brother would be the one to pay the price... Again.

Chaos would occur and Baas Tech's procedures would immediately and quickly evacuate any and all personnel wanting to leave. Leo would be able to get out fast. I had to trust him.

Leo told the Baas Tech staff that I had broken my hip while bouldering at Yosemite so I would be bedridden. He was there in my place. We would video chat once in a while, when the internet was up. He'd be in the medical tent, just checking in to let me know that things were smooth sailing. There was nothing of note until the third or fourth phone call when I started to see Dr. Laurent in the background.

She saw Leo, and she flashed her white-toothed smile. She waved her elegant slender hand. Leo smiled back and whispered a gentle "Goodnight" to her.

"What's going on there?" I asked him when she was out of the frame.

"What do you mean?" He asked too quickly. His voice was too high. He was feigning innocence.

"Why do you look like that?"

"Look like *what?*"

"Like you want to ask her out!"

He gave me a quizzical expression like I was being ridiculous. Then he rolled his eyes. "It's getting late. I'm going to head to bed. I'm all set. I'll call you."

This would be our last conversation before he went after the target. Before all hell would break loose out there.

"Okay," I said slowly, that sense of dread coming into my stomach again. A sense that everything was about to change, and the world would be turned upside down. It was that sword of Damocles. I was waiting for that horsehair to snap. "Don't forget to eat."

CHAPTER TWENTY-TWO

Los Angeles, California, USA

There was a pounding on the door, like a SWAT team trying to break in as Geordie and I quietly sipped coffee in the living room. We looked at one another, then back at the door.

The knocking started again.

"For fuck's sake, open up, I know you're in there!" The voice sounded vaguely familiar.

"A'right man, calm down," Geordie said, getting up from his seat.

When he opened the door, a most unwelcome face appeared. Brett Bradley. He barged his way in.

"Callum MacLachlan, you need to get to Barstow right now." Behind him was a short girl with black hair pulled into a high ponytail. Her eyes were heavy lined with black, and her lipstick was a deep, near-black violet. She wore black from head to toe, her billowing simple long-sleeved shirt over black jeans, and heavy combat boots on her feet. She was staring and typing on a tablet, and didn't look up as she followed Brett in.

"And why would I do that?" I asked, putting my coffee down and coming to my feet.

"Because Müller just got into the country." He put his hands in his pocket and arched a thick brow, staring at me. A moment passed and no one spoke.

I really want to knock this twat on his arse.

"By your blank expressions, I guess I'll have to break it down Barney-style for you, huh?" He looked over at the girl with him and they shared a rueful, knowing smile. He continued, "My sources tell me that he knows Lea is the Ferryman and is out for your buddy, Rashid's, ten-million-dollar bounty."

I straightened. Geordie glanced at me.

A million different questions went through my mind. How did he know? Was he a bad guy? Was he with the Americna government? Was he part of the many alphabet agencies out of Washington, DC? Who was he with? How did he know who the Ferryman was? Who is this fucking guy?

I wiped my face with my hand and decided to start from the beginning, "Is Brett Bradley your real name?"

"Seriously?" he asked, his face incredulous. "No. My real name's Chad Chadington. And I like Crossfit." He shook his head in complete disbelief. "Is this the rapier wit you get from being in MI6?"

"I was never in MI6, so I wouldn't know." I shrugged.

"Right." He tilted his head and looked at the girl. "Obviously the SAS didn't recruit for brains."

The girl sat down on the sofa, still not looking up from her tablet.

"This is Jubilee," Brett said.

"Hello, lass," Geordie went to sit beside her and did a double take when he saw her screen.

"She's my daughter," Brett scowled and glared at Geordie, "so keep your distance or they'll never find your body."

"Dieter Müller is landing in LAX right now," The girl interjected, not reacting to any of the side conversations. "And my sources indicate that he knows that he's here for Lea Bonifacio." She continued to type, type, type. "She's in the Mojave Desert, at their solar farm."

The girl smirked and looked up from under her eyelashes. The expression would have looked demure on anyone else, but with her dark lipstick, she looked mischievous. Geordie was leaning towards her, his elbows on his lap, watching as she continued to type away. Geordie was watching her face with fascination.

"How do you know where she is?" I asked.

"We put a tracker on their car," Brett said condescendingly. "Keep up, man."

I wanted to grab him by the throat. This arsehole had been following my woman.

"Why are you telling me?"

"Because I don't want her dead." He leaned forward, his eyes boring into me. "Even though you were supposed to kill her, I saw your googly eyes at the dinner table. You don't want her dead either." Brett paced across the room and stared out the large windows, slipping his hands out of his pockets and staring at his palms. "I'd happily kill Müller, based on what I know about him, but I don't have a kill order. I don't have any top cover. But you..." He looked at me, his finger pointing between my eyes. "You always have top cover, don't you?"

My spine straightened. It wasn't strictly true, but Caledonia Security could body swerve their way out of most things. Even an unsanctioned killing. He knew too much.

"Who are you with?" My eyes narrowed to slits. *Who the fuck was this guy?*

"I'm an independent contractor, and I work directly for certain government agencies. That's all you need to know." He put his hands back in his pockets.

"Müller just landed and he ordered a rental car on his phone." The girl sounded completely bored. "I have a make, model and license plate I can send to you by encrypted text."

"My phone doesn't..." I started.

"Not yours," she interrupted, looking up at me. Her eyes turned to Geordie sitting beside her, and he leaned back as if she was about to strike him. "His."

"How do you know my phone number, lass?" Geordie laid his accent down thick. He smirked at her. I knew that smirk– he was flirting with her.

She went back to her tablet, seemingly disinterested in us again.

"What's your interest in Lea?" I asked Brett, who finally looked up from his fascination with his own hands.

"Nothing romantic," he said, his palms out to me in a surrendering gesture, "I was hired to confirm that she and her brother were the assassins, build rapport, and try to bring her in to do some jobs for the stars and stripes. But confirming that they were the Ferryman took a while. Everything we had was circumstantial until recently."

"Rapport?" My eyebrows shot up. "I don't think you were going about it right."

Brett shrugged. "I thought that she'd go for the looks, and the attitude. A lot of them do." He looked almost sheepish. "By the time I realized that wouldn't work, I was stuck as Brett. We were going to change tactics soon."

"She hates you, though." I was flabbergasted that this was the technique he had chosen.

"Hate's a strong word." His smile turned cocky. "I'm sure hate can turn to *lust* if I just unload my new *crossfit bod* on her. Show her some abs."

I lunged at him, my fist up, ready to punch his face. He laughed, his hands up to defend himself.

"I'm kidding, dude! Relax!"

Jubilee looked up momentarily, saw me within inches of rearranging his face, then looked back down on her tablet.

"He's picked up his car and he's leaving," she interjected. "You now have the information in your system."

Geordie got up, went to his room, and came out with his phone in his hand.

"I have it." He looked at me, waved his phone, and said, "Though I don't know how. This isn't a public number, and I go out of my way to make sure no one has it."

He eyed the girl suspiciously. She looked up, and her heavily lined eyes blinked at him.

"You weren't very good at it." Then she turned back to her task. "We should go."

She stood up, her tablet turned off and put away.

"Where are you off to, man?" Geordie asked, looking at me from behind his cup.

"To get her."

"Are you sure you want to do this?" He put down his laptop and looked at me. "She stabbed you. She's a killer."

"We're all killers," I growl impatiently.

"I'm not," Jubilee said, matter-of-factly. "At least I'm pretty sure I'm not."

Geordie blinked at her, then shook his head as if shaking the cobwebs from his brain.

"Aye, maybe. But she's a murderer." Geordie said that last word with malice. "Are ye just thinking with yer wee badger?" he asked.

"No!" I didn't need to think about that. Yes, Lea was attractive. Yes, she was, inevitably, going to be mine. But that was not what this was about. "I'll analyze this later. I have to go."

"There's more to this than you guys see," Brett called to me as I walked away. "She's not the bad guy. Not this time."

"You're looking for a black Toyota sedan," Jubilee sounded exasperated. "In case anyone actually cares to catch the bad guy..." Her sigh spoke volumes about what she thought of us.

I didn't have time to answer either of these interlopers. There'd be time later. Right now, I had to get to my Atalanta.

I left the three of them in the hotel, slamming the door shut behind me and strode to the elevator. The few seconds it took for it to arrive were too long. The ride down was excruciating.

I got into the rental car parked in the hotel's garage. It was a blue BMW 8 series with a black interior, brand new and with the scent of freshly uphol-stered leather and all the adhesives and plastics used in modern cars.

The roar of the engine was music to my ears as I got into the I-10 East to the 1-15 North. It was a simple route, and I kept my eyes peeled for a black Toyota. I passed a few on the road, but a peek inside showed that uptight Swiss. I was an hour out from her bunker when Geordie called.

Clicking the center console, his voice came through the speakers.

"A'right, man. He's only about ten minutes ahead of you. At the rate you're going, you'll be there a few minutes after he does. I think there's a manhole that's the entrance to their bunker. I wish I could be certain that was it, but it just looks like a hole in the ground. I'll ping the coordinates to you now."

I heard my phone chime, assuming those were the coordinates.

I couldn't be sure, but I thought I heard Brett and Jubilee talking in the background.

"I'm putting you on speaker so that you can hear what this lass is saying," Geordie said, and I heard the static coming over the line before I heard Jubilee's voice.

"Müller signed up for the Foreign Legion under the name Isa de la Croix. He gained French citizenship and was living in Switzerland. Your colleague, Hugo Martin, couldn't get the man's records from the French, but he pressed on a contact in France's Secret Service and found that he had been indicted by the International Criminal Tribunal for the Former Yugoslavia. He has dark world contacts and has received several donations to an offshore account from a mysterious benefactor. He's probably complicit in hiring the Ferryman to take out Rashid Junior." She said it all so robotically, like she was reciting a grocery list. "Your friend Hugo is about to send you an email confirming what I've said about his service record."

"How do you know that?" Geordie's voice pitched high, incredulous.

"I hacked your system."

"That's impossible. I designed that system myself!"

"It's possible." She didn't match his tone but continued in her dry voice, "I did it."

There was a ping on my phone. I had, indeed, received an email. I was sure that was exactly what that girl said it was.

"Un-fucking-believable!" Geordie had probably read the email and confirmed that Jubilee penetrated our supposedly impenetrable communication systems. We'd need to discuss that at a later date.

"Can you handle all of that for me, Geordie? I can't deal with this now."

"A'right, man." His voice turned grave, lowered as though this could be our last conversation. "Good luck. Say hi to the wee lass for me."

"*Tapadh leat.*" Thank you, in Scots.

I could hear him breathing on the other end of the line. The Scots meant more than just a common language but was everything that was common between the two of us.

"Of course," he finally said. "Chocolate is thicker than blood."

"And scotch is better than chocolate."

CHAPTER TWENTY-THREE

THE BUNKER FELT COLD and hollow. My fingers tapped on the desk, and it echoed from the stone walls like the endless clicking of a clock. The satellite phone was in my hand, and its silence was so loud that it shook my brain. The winds were howling through the rocks and canyons above and I could hear the chuffing of distant coyotes.

Something was wrong. I just knew it. I felt it in the dropping pit of my stomach.

Was Leo hurt? Was he dead? Did the mission fail?

How am I going to live without him? When this has all been my fault...

I was laying low because Leo - not Callum! - told me to. Because I owed him a little cooperation.

The phone chimed. With shaking hands, I pull the black brick of a phone out of the pocket of my large cargo pants and place it at my ear.

"Ano?" *What?*

I closed my eyes so that I could try to hear everything through the static. I heard rhythmic chopping sounds like the blades of a helicopter. Voices shouted in the background. Random clicks and sounds. It took a moment before a loud, clear voice, as familiar to me as my own finally spoke. "I'll be home for dinner."

Then he clicked off. Code for the mission was done.

I sighed and let out a loud exhale. I expected to feel relief but I didn't.

The sword above my head had not been removed.

There remained a chill in my spine like someone walked over my grave.

I had to get out of this underground bunker. I needed to breathe. I crawled up the ladder and out into the air. The sun was setting, and the air was frigid and dry. I started to pace the dessert and it's hard, crusty sand. A thin layer of moon dust kicked up around me as I walked. The slight wind that rode through the canyon blew into my hair and filled my senses with white noise.

It also carried with it a human sound. The kind of metal clicking. A man-made sound that I hadn't made.

I was being watched.

I scanned the ground at my feet. Nothing. Then I looked about ten feet ahead of me, turning over my shoulder. I saw nothing there but the dust flying over the hard, caked, and dry desert ground. Then I looked twenty feet away. There were canyons on either side of me, funneling from east to west, channeling the wind. Then I scanned the distance looking for a tell-tale sign of... I wasn't sure what.

I was looking for the shine, like the sun reflecting on the glass of a scope. Or a black piece of metal common in weapons, nestled hidden by the sun-bleached rocks. I was scanning for an unfamiliar face, back and forth in the distance.

I waited, unmoving so that I could hear everything.

Then there it was. The faintest *click*.

I took a deep breath and chanted an old phrase in my head that I learned in the army.

I'm up...

I identified the nearest bounder that I could get between me and that click.

He sees me...

I ran, pumping my arms and legs, the momentum taking me to the ground.

I'm down.

I landed on the ground, my back to the boulder.

The shot didn't land far from me. The dust kicked up from the bullet's impact just a couple feet from where I had been. The noise echoed around the rocks until it faded out in the distance.

The coyotes went silent.

"Come out, come out, Ferryman," a voice sing-songed. He sounded like the Joker in Batman, but with a faint Balkan accent.

There was that sword of Damocles, the string snipped, and falling into my skull.

I didn't have a gun on me. I was in the middle of the Mojave Desert. The most dangerous thing out here was a slightly feral donkey. I hadn't thought about it. That carelessness might cost me my life.

All I had on me was my butterfly knife.

I felt it in my hip pocket and snapped it open, blade out.

I glanced further toward the canyons at my side. The place was rocky. Interconnected wadis, the dried out riverbeds, ran east to west. Whoever was out there was between me and the closed hatch of the bunker.

I could try to sneak up on him and kill him. That didn't have a great chance of success since I had no element of surprise.

I could take him head on, but that didn't seem wise.

Turning away from where I crouched, I skirted around the rocks, keeping a low profile. I tilted my head to peer around a little red rock. I heard movement and pulled back just as a bullet flew where my head had been, sending a cloud of red dust in the air.

"Are you alright, sweetheart?" That evil voice again. *I fucking hate endearments. If I get my hands on him, I'll make sure he dies slowly.*

I needed to bait him. Right now, I had no clue where he was, and I couldn't pop my head up to look.

I cupped my hand around my mouth.

"I'm peachy," I projected out to some rocks, knowing that it would echo down the canyon and distort where I was.

I swiftly moved to another rock as the echoes of my voice faded away. He fired, the bullet landing several feet away, near the rock I had hidden behind. I looked at where the bullet landed on the ground. The hole, its angle, told me where he was firing from. I moved away to try to get more rocks and cover between me and that psycho.

I controlled my breathing as best as I could. My pulse was loud in my temples. I was losing focus. I was losing control. I inhaled deep and waited. There was silence. A pause. He wasn't moving.

I heard his voice again, laughing like a fucking psychopath.

"You couldn't just do your job and make it look like an accident." It was impossible for me to tell what direction he came from.

The sound was bouncing off of everything. This was the most ridiculous, and dangerous, game of Marco Polo I had ever played.

A rude memory flashed before my eyes.

Me and Leo, toddlers, on our parent's shoulders in the community pool on a hot summer day.

I shut my eyes and willed those thoughts away. I wasn't going to let my life flash before my eyes. It wasn't going to be my time. Not now.

"You've been very hard to track down, Lea Bonifacio. But when we got that serial number from the scalpel...well. It was all just a matter of time."

I knew it was a mistake. I shouldn't have left the scalpel.

But if I had pulled that scalpel out of Callum, he'd be dead.

I didn't regret letting him live. Even if it cost me my life. Callum was probably worth it. Maybe I should have fucked him while I had a chance. I definitely wouldn't have regretted that.

Then another thought.

His hands on my dress, ripping it open. Him, cutting the wires to the microphone and feed. His lips on mine.

I shook that away too. I needed to get my head in the game.

"You've caused a real headache, you know. But you fell short of your reputation."

I cupped my hands around my mouth and yelled towards the bare face of a rock several feet away, hoping that the extra bounce of my voice would add enough confusion for him to make another mistake.

"I don't think we've met. Who are you?"

Another burst. A bullet whizzed overhead and struck the rock. I knew where he was. I continued to skirt and climb, to put additional distance between us.

If I could just get closer to my car, or to the bunker... There'd be guns there. I knew I could win in a fair fight.

But the distance between me and the bunker had nothing but low brush. No cover, just a little bit of concealment. It was my only hope.

I crawled on my belly, slowly so as not to make noise. If I could just...

I heard footsteps. I felt the shadow looming overhead.

Looking down, I saw that the ground had gotten dark. He was standing over me.

Time's up.

In an instant, I felt regret. Regret for the danger I was leaving my parents in. Regret that I pulled Leo into this life. Regret that I was leaving this world alone.

I hadn't given much thought to dying. I wondered if it would hurt. Would he shoot me in the head, or would he aim for my stomach and leave me to bleed out and die in slow, painful agony?

I raised my head to him, staring down the barrel of his Desert Eagle. Of course, it was a Desert Eagle. Large, heavy and awkward. The weapon of limp-dicked men.

He should be embarrassed by that.

I hope he aimed for my head.

Things slowed down. His grin tightened into scorn and hate. His hand tensed before his finger started pulling the trigger ever so slowly. His whole body quaked with gleeful anticipation.

This was my final moment. I had one chance, one moment of retaliation. These would be my last words.

"I'll see you in hell."

Click.

CHAPTER TWENTY-FOUR

I turned off the freeway, onto a dirty road. I parked, grabbed an M-4 from the trunk and slung it over my shoulder. I gripped its familiar weight tight to my body. With the earpiece in, I could hear Geordie's voice as he gave me the information from his satellite images.

"Head northwest." I looked at the sky, looked at the sun, then blindly obeyed his directions. We didn't have time to launch a drone, but we were near Fort Irwin, the U.S. Army Post, so there were things in the sky that he could tap into with his *special* skills.

"She's on the move, but it looks like there's limited cover. He's shot at her twice, but she looks unharmed," he coldly narrated. "She's low crawling around him and heading your way."

I took a deep breath and started to jog, keeping my steps light and silent as possible.

"You'll see him at your two o'clock. You might be able to see her at your nine." I focused on his words and hurried my steps. My stomach was in my throat, and I felt the adrenaline coursing through my fingers that managed to not twitch by the grace of decades of training.

She's not gone, I thought as I steadied my breathing. Slow is smooth and smooth is fast.

I popped behind a red rock not much taller than my hips. He was two hundred meters from me down the narrow canyon valley.

Müller's back was to me. He was scanning, his two hands on his pistol out, shoulders squared. He was looking for *her*. His lips were drawn in a maniacal smile. It was the most emotion I had ever seen on him. I could practically feel the excitement vibrating from his body.

He was a predator close to his kill.

The wind came at me from their direction and carried their voices so I heard them clear as day.

"I don't think we've met. You know, you sound like a Bond villain. Don't you know that once you start your exposition, you start the countdown to your own death?" her voice dripped with venom, fearless as always.

He fired. It hit a rock that wasn't far from her. He shot at the echo of her voice instead of at her. But it was too close for comfort.

I was as silent as the grave. Bringing the weapon up on top of the rock, I stabilized it. I got him in the crosshairs, his salt and pepper hair shining under the harsh sun. He was moving towards her.

The wind was working in my favor, and carrying the sound of my breath and movements away from them. I clicked my selector switch from safe to semi. My finger was on the trigger and I breathed in to steady myself.

I only had one chance to do this.

I can't do it.

It had been years since I was asked to kill someone. Not since I left the service. I started a security firm to protect lives, not take them, and here I was, about to kill for a woman. I was ready to be judge, jury and executioner.

Müller's head turned, his lips pulled back into a snarl. He'd tracked her. He saw her with her head in the ground, blindly low crawling towards the bunker. She was coming closer toward me.

With a renewed energy, Müller moved. His shadow loomed over her. She noticed. Then she stilled and raised her head.

I expected fear. Pleading. Anything else but what I saw. For a moment, she blinked in silence. Then one eyebrow rose and she smiled. More accurately, she snarled, her teeth bared, her eyes sparkling with cruel amusement.

Her voice rang out loud and clear. "I'll see you in hell."

His finger tightened on his Desert Eagle…

Müller heard a sound, his head jerking just a millimeter in my direction before I took the shot. The bullet went through his head, and he fell to his knees before collapsing on top of her, his blood splattering across the sand.

I ran to them.

She wasn't moving.

Was I too late? Had he fired first? Fuck, why did I hesitate?

I pulled the heavy, limp body off of her. I heaved and tossed him like a sack of flour off to the side, then knelt before her. She was covered in blood. Her eyes were open.

She was still. So fucking still. Her eyes stared up at the sky, unblinking.

"Fuck," I cupped her face in my hands, my thumps trying to wipe away the splatters of blood, but only made it worse. The red painted further into her skin. "Lea? Lea!"

She was cold. Her skin was clammy.

I couldn't hear her breathing.

Then she blinked. Her chest heaved.

"Can you hear me? Lea!"

Another blink. Her eyes shifted to me. With strange, twitchy, shaking hands, she touched her torso. Then her face. Then she looked down on herself.

"I'm not hit," Her voice was weak. "The blood's not mine, so that's good."

I put my hands on her face, wiping away the streaks of crimson. It was in her hair. On her chest. It was everywhere and my shaking hands wiped over her skin looking for holes.

"Fuck." I was relieved. I drew her to me, bringing her face into my chest. "Thank God."

She's alive. Relief waved through my body. I wrapped her in my arms. I placed a kiss on top of her head. She hesitantly put her hands on my biceps. I thought she would push me away, but instead, she clung to me.

"Hey, there." She pushed me away a few inches so that I could look down into her serene face. "I'm okay."

She reached up with her blood-covered hands and smiled. I felt the moistness of the dead man's blood on my cheeks.

Her eyes were clear. No tears. She was comforting *me* with a puzzled expression on her face.

"Let me up," she gently said.

I pulled away from her and she came to her feet. She looked down at her cargo pants and dusted at the specks of blood as if to wipe them off. But it just smeared further and she sighed in annoyance.

Her hands patted her body again, from her neck to her chest, and onto her face.

"I'm okay," she repeated. Then she turned to face me again. "Thank you."

She sounded cheery when she said it.

I looked at the red stain, absorbing into the dirt at her feet.

"This is where you say... *you're welcome*." She said it in a playful whisper.

"You're covered in blood," I told her, as if she wasn't aware.

"I know. I've got to go to the bunker to shower it off." She looked at my hands, then to my shirt. She wiped her hand over my white button-down. "Now you're covered, too."

She looked at the body at our feet. Müller's hair was flying in the wind, but the rest of him was as still as the stones.

"We need to get rid of his body." Her hands were on her waist as she looked around at the desert around us. "We can't bury him here. It's too dry. The body will take centuries to decompose." She looked up at the sky that had gone from vibrant reds and oranges to dark blue, heralding the start of night. "Any ideas?"

I placed my hands on either side of her face again.

I had no answers and no ideas except for my desire to look at her and feel her. To know that she was real, and alive, and that her skin was warm beneath my hands.

"Not that you need to know this...but there are no other threats in the area. You're clear," Geordie's voice said into my earpiece, adding a little chuckle.

"Stop watching. I'll call if I need you again."

"I have a suggestion," an American voice came over the line. Brett Bradley.

I groaned. Lea couldn't hear what I heard, so she quirked her head.

"Your *boyfriend* Brett is on the line," I told her.

Her nose wrinkled at the word boyfriend.

"What the hell is he doing there?" she mumbled.

"He contracts with your feds." I smiled at her. "It's a long story, but you have a stalker, love."

She looked disgusted, perplexed, and very annoyed.

"Alright, assholes, I'm offering you a suggestion on how to dispose of the body." His voice sounded annoyed. "I'm calling your phone. Put me on speaker."

"Fat chance," I told him.

The phone in my pocket buzzed. I pulled it out and the name "STUD MUFFIN" came up on the caller ID. *What the bloody hell?*

Lea saw it, then looked at me in question.

"I didn't fuckin' do that," I protested.

I clicked the phone and placed it on speaker. Without so much as a hello, he started speaking.

"Your relationship is far too young for you to be making decisions for her." Brett's jovial voice was annoying as it came over the line. "Is this really what you want, Lea? A control freak like this? It's only going to get worse from here."

"What's going on?" she mouthed to me.

"He says he has a solution for the body." I ran a finger down her cheek again. "Do you want to hear him out? You don't have to, darling. I'll gladly hang up on him."

She took in a deep breath, looked into the distance and thought for a moment before turning back to me. She shrugged. "I guess I'll hear him out."

"Well thank you ever so," the voice on the line chimed in, sarcastically.

"He flirts with you, then I'll kill him," I whispered to her.

"I heard that!" Brett said.

Lea and I laughed in unison. She idly placed her hand to my chest, stroking my shirt with her bloodied palm leaving even more streaks along the silk.

"I can get a disposal team out there, but you two have to make yourself scarce," Brett instructed. His voice lost any of its normal personality. He was all business. He was less grating that way. "Jump in the bunker for a couple of hours. It's best if they don't see you and you don't see them."

"Okay, and what will it cost me?" she asked, as though she was negotiating the price of a lemon in a used car lot.

"A marker, sweet cheeks. That's it," Brett chirped. "Some time soon, I'm going to need the Ferryman for something, and you give it, no questions asked. In return, I keep this whole mess away from the feds. Sound good?"

That didn't sound good to me at all. I'd rather bury the body myself than have her owing that prick a damn thing. I was about to open my mouth to tell her that exact thing but she beat me to it.

"The marker is for me," she said firmly. "Not my brother. Only me."

"Copy that," Brett said. "I'll even go a step further and promise that you'll be working on the side of the angels. When I ask for my favor, you'll be working with the good guys."

She rolled her eyes. "Everyone thinks they're the good guys."

"Honey bun, I can guarantee *I* am the good guys." That crap personality was back in full force. "There's a bigger game happening here." His voice softened. "I don't think you know what you're dealing with. I'm the guy you want on your side. I promise you."

"How would I know you'll keep your word?"

"That's the million-dollar question, lamb chop," he said. "How do I know you'll keep yours and you won't kill my guys when they come to dispose of that Alpine dick? We gotta work on that trust, babe."

She recoiled from all the endearment. The man was getting on my last nerve too.

"We can start by being a little nicer at the dinner table, don't you think?" Brett asked. "I'm harmless, after all."

His flirting made me want to crush the phone in my hand. But it wasn't my place to speak on her behalf. It wasn't on me to protect her or tell her what to do... no matter how much I wanted to.

"How long will it take? The disposal?" she finally asked.

"Two hours." Brett mumbled something and faded back on the line. "Right Jubilee?" He didn't direct that at us. "Yeah, two hours. Stay down for two and a half just in case."

Lea looked up at me with a seductive, coquettish smile.

"I'm sure I could find a way to amuse myself."

CHAPTER TWENTY-FIVE

The place smelled like brick, circulated air, and WD-40. There was a comfortable chill in the air that relaxed me considerably. Military-style metal shelves lined the cement walls. Green and black duffel bags, probably full of weapons, lined the room.

On one end were blackened monitors. On the other were plywood walls, obviously put in recently. I could hear running water in the room Lea had walked to.

I was livid. I didn't like that she had given that bellend, Brett, a marker. I didn't want him to have any reason to contact her. Not without me around to run interference. I needed to find a way to insert myself without violating her privacy or her trust. I didn't trust that California douche bag, and she didn't have any fear or sense of self-preservation.

She pulled on something inside me that I had tamped down in my years outside of the service. I had become a consummate gentleman since my time in MI-6, with clear moral lines that I stayed between, where it was safe. I kept a cordial distance from women, even Pippa.

I wanted to replace Brett's tracker on her car with my own. I wanted to put a trojan horse on her phone. I wanted to embed a tracker in her skin so I knew she was alive, and safe, and I'd never be more than a few minutes away and could wrap her in my arms in a second.

This possession, this ferocity, had been simmering under the surface and she brought it out of me.

I should just let her shower.

I should be a gentleman and stay far away. But the longer I waited for her, the more my feet moved towards the sound of water, where I knew she'd be naked under the stream.

I tried – *I truly did!* – to stop myself. But my hand rested on the door separating me from that bathroom. I turned the latch and pushed it open without meaning to, as though something else had taken control of my body.

The steam billowed and there she was like a goddess in the mist, just a silhouette through a translucent shower curtain. She knew I was there, but she didn't pause or look back, her hands continuing their massage of her neck and shoulders.

I pushed the curtain aside and saw her in all her glory. She faced away from me, her hair plastered to her head, little streaks of soap dripped down the muscles of her toned back, to her slim waist and perfect, round arse.

I never knew I had a physical "type" before. Sure, the women of my past had been slim and conventionally attractive, but there was something about her tiny, tightly built frame and the way her muscles moved under her soft skin that made me feral.

Even her tan lines appealed to me. It lightened on her shoulders where her halter blocked the sun. Across her bicep was another line from her t-shirt. The lightest skin was at her intimate parts, on her breasts and buttocks where a bikini would be. It was like a beacon, lighting my way home.

It felt dirty to see that pale skin, and she hadn't even turned around yet.

Cheap, square, white tiles surrounded her in the small shower. There was a drain under her feet where the blood, water, and soap swirled like a whirlpool.

I didn't interrupt her. Not yet.

I was looking at a dream. I was in the presence of a fantasy that I didn't know I had.

I pulled off my clothes and dropped them where I stood. She didn't react to the sound of my belt clanking on the floor, though I knew she heard it.

I stepped into the steam, reaching out my hands. I was rock hard, and I wanted nothing more than to pin her against a wall and violently take her, but that would be a disservice to us both.

Not when the anticipation and the uncertainty was so delicious.

I'd had my hands on her three times before. Once, she stabbed me. The next, I nearly ravaged her in the backroom of a bar. Then, I held her blood-covered body to me just a few minutes ago.

This would be the fourth, and it would change everything. I was ready for that change. I was ready for what this touch would begin, but I wanted to delay it. To prolong the sweetness of wanting before this little jasmine would become mine.

It was a while before I realized that she had stopped moving.

Our breathing synchronized. I moved forward and my fingers grazed the dimples on her lower back. She gasped. I held still. I had to ask the real questions now.

"Were you serious?" I asked her, barely loud enough to be heard over the cascading water.

"Serious about what?" her voice was husky and uncertain.

"About your safe word." I let my fingers graze right to the top of that tan line at the top of that peach-shaped rear. "Or were you just pulling my dick? Because what I want is...a lot. I'm not proud of it, but I'm too old to deny what I need."

"What do you need?"

"Rough," I growled. "To fuck you violently."

"I can take violence." Her voice was amused, but she still wouldn't turn to look at me. "What are you afraid of?"

"Hurting you."

She laughed, throwing her head back slightly.

"I've made you bleed." Her voice lowered in a challenge, "Do your worst."

That was permission enough. I couldn't wait another moment. I put my hands on her hips and turned her towards me. Her eyes were bright, amused, and filled with lust. I put my hand around her ribs, digging my fingers into her skin, feeling her taut sinews flex. I needed her to feel it. To feel the sting. To feel the bruises forming. I needed to mark her.

I searched her face one last time. I searched for any hint of uncertainty or fear. Anything that told me that she did not want this as much as I did.

"I want to fuck you," I said against her cheek, "but you already know that I don't have a condom."

"I'm clean."

"I know that. I've seen your medical records and I know you're on the shot."

"That's fucked up." She chuckled and quirked an eyebrow. "I've seen yours, too. You have a lot of bullet wounds."

"I need your permission to do what I want."

"What do you want?"

"You know what I want."

"Fucking say it. Say it in words," She commanded. "I like it when you do."

I did. I said it against her ear, "I want to fuck you. I want to fill that sweet cunt of yours."

"That wasn't a question."

"If you don't use your safe word soon, I'm going right ahead." She had no idea what kind of danger she was in. "Last chance, *darling*."

I put all my lust, my need, my heat that bubbled beneath the surface into that endearment. She smirked and bit her lower lip.

I roared! It echoed off the tiles and I saw her eyes go wide. But it wasn't fear. Her lips spread in a smile, the kind that screamed for me to take and take and take...

I closed my eyes and took one last breath. One last moment.

When I opened my eyes, I felt it snap. My control. My discipline.

My fingers dug into her ribs again, pulling her towards me until her taut, brown nipples pressed against my chest.

"Times up," I said into her ear.

I picked her up, and her legs automatically wrapped around my waist. The tip of my cock rested snuggly near her entrance. I slammed her back against the tiles, and the cheap porcelain cracked under the force.

She didn't flinch. She didn't show weakness. Her hand came to my jaw, her thumb on one side, and her fingers digging into my opposite cheek. Her eyes were wide, her teeth bared.

My ferocious, little goddess.

I reached between us and placed my tip at her wet and warm entrance. Her fingers dug harder into my face. She was fighting me. My beautiful girl was challenging me and it made my cock bob, wanting to thrust into her until she was crying my name.

I thrust into her, and her eyes rolled back into her head, shuddering beautifully in my arms.

She forced her eyes open and looked at me. She bared those teeth again. This little predator woman...

"Is that it?" she mocked.

I thrust into the hilt. She whimpered as I brought my mouth to hers. Our teeth and tongues clashed violently like we were sparring. She wanted to give me control, but she wouldn't make it easy for me.

Still, I had to slow down. She was so small and light that she strangled my cock. I felt her throbbing from the inside as I found my rhythm, sliding in and out of her.

I had to slow down if I wanted her more than once today. I needed to mold her to me slowly so that I didn't hurt her in a way that would prevent a second, or third, round.

Fuck! This was the woman I have been waiting for.

I pulled her away from the wall until she was held up by nothing but my embrace and my throbbing cock. Broken tiles fell to the floor, clinking like falling glass. My hand supported her ass as I gently thrust in and out of her.

She groaned, her head collapsing into the spot between my shoulder and her neck.

"That's right, darling. Give yourself to me."

"Never." Her whimper was weak. Half-hearted. Her resistance was crumbling.

"Come for me," I demanded as I bit her neck, sucking the delicate skin between my teeth. Her hips thrust harder, driving me deeper. Her heat was pulsing, tighter and tighter. Her mouth opened, her head fell back and she screamed, her nails dragging down my back. I knew she drew blood, and I'm sure it mingled with the hot water down my skin.

Her cry was a beautiful, desperate, passionate scream. Her cunt pulsed around me, tightening with her ecstasy.

She fell apart in my arms, held up by nothing but my body. The water cascaded over her breasts. With the shower spray, the steam and her hair plastered to her tanned skin, she looked ethereal and pleasured like a nymph.

Her head fell forward onto my shoulder. I wrapped my arms around her, her legs shaking and unsteady around my waist. My cock held the little goddess up, exactly where she belonged.

She had obeyed me. Fuck! Obedience from a woman like this… that was power, and I felt it surging through my body. I was high on it. I needed more.

I blindly reached with one arm to shut the water off. The steam cooled away. The cold air hit our skin in a matter of seconds, and I felt her shiver.

"Where's the bed?" I demanded as I walked out of the bathroom with her small body still wrapped around me.

She pointed at a wooden door that was propped open near the bathroom. I pushed past it and brought us inside. There was no lock or doorknob to keep it closed. The walls didn't go all the way up to the ceiling. The plywood walls were bare. There were nails in the wall. On those nails rested an M-4 with a scope. On another was an AK-47 and assorted other weapons. The bed was made of a wooden platform and thin mattress. On top of it was a scratchy, green woolen army issued blanket with the black "U.S." stamp on it.

With much effort, I gently lay her on the bed, breaking our connection.

"You're still hard," she whispered, her eyes becoming lucid, seeming to see my body for the first time.

I grinned at her. She was still dripping wet, and limp from her orgasm.

"You'll give me another orgasm, before I get inside you again. Now, spread your legs," I demanded. She didn't move. "Do what you're told."

"I'm one and done, *sweetheart*," she chuckled, using the endearment sarcastically. "I appreciate the gesture, but you should do what you need to do."

She lay back, as if resigned to her fate. The little darling had no idea what I had in store for her.

"I said…" I crawled over her naked body to whisper in her ear. "You're going to give me one more before I continue fucking you. So do what I tell you and spread. Your. Legs."

She gasped, but obeyed. I took my time kissing down her body until my lips rested on her perfectly shaved pussy. I spread her folds apart until I could see her clit. I licked it gently, and she shivered. Then I took it in my mouth.

I wrapped my arms around her legs and pinned her hips down onto the mattress as she started to buck hard against my face. It wouldn't take her long, I could feel it in the quivering tension of her thighs. A tear trickled down from her right eye, down her temple as she was about to fall over the edge.

Fucking beautiful.

I saw the moment she surrendered. Her eyes flew open in disbelief. She gasped, looked down at me, mouth open and a pleasured scream escaped from somewhere deep in her throat. Her thighs tensed around my face and I savored her struggle. Her struggle to deny her own pleasure, to deny our connection was falling apart on my tongue, dripping down my chin.

I lapped it up, continuing to lick her until her body shuddered with a cry. She tried to push my face away, but her arms were weak and shaking.

I chuckled as I moved up her body. Her head fell to one side.

I put my hand on her cheek and tilted her head towards me. I kissed the corner of her mouth letting her taste herself on my lips.

My patience was done. I put my rock-hard cock at her entrance and entered her in one hard stroke. Her nails dug into my shoulders, and she whined at my invasion. Her pulsing, tight heat clamped down on my cock, and I knew it wouldn't take me long. I took her wrists off my shoulders and pinned them to the bed. I put my teeth onto her clavicle, biting down hard, just shy of breaking her skin. I kept thrusting and she struggled against my hold.

"Fuck!" she whimpered in disbelief. "God, I'm… I'm coming again."

"Good," I growled. "You can come with me."

She did exactly that. She crossed her ankles behind my back and held on for dear life as I pistoned inside her. I bit down on the soft, tender skin of her neck where I could still smell the hint of that jasmine perfume and took it between my teeth until I knew that my mark would stay there.

This goddess of a woman, who didn't flinch as bullets flew over her head, who was covered in blood and simply washed it all away was now mine. That thought pushed me over the edge.

I emptied inside her, knowing that we were linked forever because I would never be able to let her go.

I knew in that instant that I would have her in a Scottish winter. That I would pin her down and make love to her in Strathlachlan, by the loch, in the castle, in the woods, in the fields... everywhere.

I kissed her. Her hand reached up to stroke my cheek, her nails combing my beard.

I put my forehead to hers and took in the moment. Her breaths, the smell of her skin, her soap, the rise and fall of her breasts, and the feel of her thighs against my hips.

"You're all mine now," I told her. "I'm never letting you go."

"Oh sure," she laughed lightly. "That's reasonable."

"I'm not joking, lass." I didn't try to hide my Scottish brogue anymore. "You'll see."

When our breaths evened out, she stroked my face, staring up at me with those brown eyes. When I separated from her, she whimpered, then her limp arm pointed to where a washcloth stood on a nearby dresser. I retrieved it and wiped, slowly between her thighs. She smiled as she watched me, and I welcomed her scrutiny.

Tossing it to the floor, I came to rest on top of her again. I kissed her forehead, her cheek, and buried my face into her neck. I wrapped an arm around her shoulders and rolled us so that I was on my back, and she was pressed into my side. The wool blanket dug into my skin, but I didn't care. I liked having her curled into me. Her skin was warm, the air was cold.

I finally looked around the room.

There was a small black frame on the nightstand. In it was a man with a straw fedora and white shirt, smiling a crooked smile at whoever was taking the photo. He looked like he was about to jokingly wink.

"Who's that man in that picture?" I ran my fingers up and down the pattern of bluing skin on her ribs.

"Uncle Leopold– Tito Leo." Her voice was thick, tired, and satisfied. "He's how I started in this business."

"Tell me about him," I said against her wet hair as my fingers traced the beautiful bite mark I left on her neck.

"You really want to know?" She propped herself up on her elbow and looked down at me, her head tilted.

"I do." I wanted to know every little thing about her.

"I had just gotten out of the Army. My grandfather died, so we all went to the Philippines for the funeral." She took a finger to the scalpel scar on my shoulder. "Tito Leo took us to the bars to party because...that's the kind of man he was." She stroked my chest, playing with the course, red hair that grew between my pecs. "My mother says he never quit gallivanting around, going disco-disco." She affected a light accent, mocking her mother's voice. "Anyway, this one cop became... fixated on me that night. Maybe it's because I'm American, and maybe he was just a terrible guy. Cops in the Philippines under this president are...corrupt. When I rejected him, he threatened my family. He said that once I was gone, he could hurt my cousins with impunity because the police own the law. And it's true. Stick some drugs on someone, and you're justified in killing them."

She propped herself up on one elbow, resting her cheek on her hand. She continued to rub my chest and I felt the sweet effects of the afterglow. Her eyes scanned down my body to my satisfied cock. The blood drained from my head as my todger reacted to her attention. I closed my eyes to try to control it. This was not a time to become aroused.

"I pretended to give in. I walked him down the Pasig River on the way back to where our family lived. He said he lived that way." Her hands started to stroke up and down my abs, stopping just at the apex of my Adonis belt. "Anyway, he was drunk. It wasn't hard to overpower him. I held his head under the plastic-covered, polluted water until he stopped moving." She looked at her hands, tilting her head. "Tito Leo followed us. Do you know what he said after he helped get rid of the body?"

I shook my head, coming up onto my elbow to look closer at her face. I expected some emotion there, but she was as serene as a swan on the glassy lake.

"He said that I could have done it better. It turns out that his persona was a ruse." She smiled as she shared this little secret. "He brought me into the business. Then Leo joined us when I couldn't hide what I was doing from him."

She lay silent for a moment, staring at her uncle's photo. "Do you ever have trouble sleeping?" she asked out of the blue.

"After a kill? It's been a while, but...no. My kills were mostly in a time of war."

She hummed in acknowledgment. She wasn't judging me. She was genuinely curious. "I've done that too. But even the ones I've been paid for, I never lost sleep. No one really pays the big bucks to off decent people, you know?"

"I suppose that makes us psychopaths."

"Oh, I'm sure I am. But my brother doesn't sleep afterwards." Her eyes became distant as she continued to look at the photograph, her hand still lightly grazing my skin.

CHAPTER TWENTY-SIX

I LAY MY HEAD on his chest, tracing a finger on the scar of his shoulder. The scar that I had given him. The mark that he would keep forever because of me. He was on his back, one arm up and under his head like a pillow. The other arm was under my head. Our legs were tangled together, and our heated skin cooled under the cold air.

His fingers lazily combed my short hair, and he kissed my forehead.

"You should come with me." He was sleepy, his eyes half closed, his voice heavy.

"To where?" I struggled to keep my eyes open as well.

"To Scotland." He smiled as if it was the most obvious thing in the world.

"What for?" I yawned.

"To see my home," he whispered. "I've seen yours, so you should see mine."

I chuckled, tracing my hand down his muscled torso to his thickening cock. He stopped me before I reached for it, flattening my hand against his stomach.

"Come see my home." He pulled on my hair until my head tilted up to look at him.

"Don't you live in a castle?" I teased.

"I have one, but I don't live there. The other's just a ruin." He didn't hear my joke. "Would you like to see it, though? We could spend a night or two there."

It wasn't lost on me that he stopped sounding British after we made love. His Scottish accent deepened his voice, and it rumbled deep in his chest.

"Sounds kinda stuffy. Do castles have air conditioning?"

"No, lass." He laughed. "We can't change the structure. It's a historic building."

"Oh?" I put on a serious face. "What a dump."

He laughed and pulled me in closer. "Will ye come with me?"

I raised my eyebrow, the double entendre clear. "I have already."

"Answer my question, love," he said softly. "You're prevaricating."

"You want me to come visit your castle? Like a princess?" I wanted to keep this light. He was taking us down a serious path that I wasn't ready for.

"Yes." His fingers moved to my ribs to touch the singing blue bruises he had marked me with. "But the best I can offer you is a barony. So, you would'na be a princess."

He drew me in closer to him. "Truthfully, I think the last princess that was at Strathlachlan might have been Kate. That was a long time ago, and before she was officially a princess."

"Kate?" I asked.

"Middleton. Wife to William." He said it so casually that it didn't register who he meant until my fatigued little mind could figure out who that was.

"William... the Prince? Balding guy? Son of Diana?" I came up onto my elbow and looked down at him, my eyebrows raised. *Is he fucking with me?*

"Aye, that one," he said it as if it was the most mundane thing.

My mouth hung open. I had been joking this whole time. I thought he was pulling my leg. Or, in his words, pulling his dick. Were there goblins and werewolves in his world too? Maybe a unicorn or two? At this point, I wouldn't be surprised.

If Kate Middleton was, at one point, a not-quite-princess, then what was I? A peasant? A pleb? A nothing?

That was it. The end of a fantasy. The final, dying flicker of that afterglow, plunging me back into the darkness I lived in.

We weren't in this together. We weren't the same. It was time for me to continue in the shithole bunker, the plywood walls, the hot, fucked up desert that I lived in.

He'd go back to his fucking castles, his mansions, his penthouses and I'd be here, driving a beat-up old car, in my polyester dresses, and knock-off shoes.

He'd go back to perfect Pippa, the fucking supermodel. And I'd end up with the guys more my speed. The guys my mom set me up with from church.

What do you expect, dumbass? You met him at a gala he attended, while you were paid to collect donation... and assassinated that one guy in the Lake.

"Where did you go, darling?" His voice pulled me from my stupor. "What's going through your head?"

His voice was sweet and gentle. He was staring at me. I closed my eyes to enjoy the sound of it. I savored it one last time before I let the other shoe drop. Before reality finally came upon me. I pulled out of his arms and started to get out of bed.

"Why are you pulling away from me?" He asked.

"We should go. They would have removed the body by now," I tried to sound even, as if this was all business.

"Are we in a fight?" his voice perked up, almost agitated.

He got up after me, still naked and gorgeous as he ran his hand through his wet hair. Fuck, he should be made into a statue.

"Speak to me. I cannot read your mind." His voice was tremendously calm, and I heard that Scottish voice disappearing, and that posh British one came back.

The haze of sex was gone. I could see clearly that nothing could happen between us from here.

We weren't just from different worlds–me a hitman, him in protection–but even our social class and our realities were completely different. What would I do? Move him into my parent's house? Would I move with him into his castle?

Fucking ridiculous.

I walked to the shelves where I kept my spare clothes. I put on an oversized shirt, and panties. I was hiding from his gaze, which burned into my back.

"I'm not pulling away," I whispered. "There's nothing to pull away from."

"Yes, you are. And yes, there is," he countered. "You are mine now."

His voice was more Scottish on that last phrase, more guttural, more demanding and it heated my skin. I wanted nothing more than to give in to him and pretend the world didn't exist and that it was only us now.

I heard him move behind me. His heat was radiating onto my skin, even through my shirt. His hands came to my waist and I heard him moan at the contact. I wanted to push into his arms but I couldn't give in to the illusion. The dreams of a little girl and castles and fairy tales weren't mine, and this one time was the most I would ever get from him.

"What's wrong, darling?" he cooed, like I was some wild horse that needed taming.

I flinched away from his hands. "I hate it when you say that."

"When I say what?"

"Darling. All of it. I fucking hate it." I tried to keep the resentment from my voice. I wanted to reign it in, but there was a pain in the pit of my stomach and I needed to lunge at him, to hurt him, to slash at him. I turned and confronted him straight on. "I hate endearments. I always have. My name is Lea. Not babe, baby, darling, honey… It's Lea. What? Have you been with so many women that you need the endearments when you forget their names?"

His brow knitted. His eyes darkened. "You think I don't know exactly who you are?" His voice was calm, but I could hear the anger brewing under the surface. "You think I would *ever* mistake you for someone else?"

His temper was rising to match my own. He was still gloriously naked, and it hurt to see that physical beauty. That perfection that would never be mine.

I rolled my eyes and walked away from him. He reached out and grabbed me by the shoulders and turned me to face him again. I wanted to fight him, but my legs were still weak. Even if he hadn't orgasmed me into compliance, I couldn't fight him when it came to brute strength alone.

But I could be defiant. I could glare. I could spew.

"Answer me, *Lea*," he emphasized my name. Not darling. Not love. Just my plain name. "I know everything about you Leonora Ascuncion Bonifacio. Make no mistake about that."

"You've seen my full name when you researched." I tried to pull away again. "That doesn't mean anything."

"Yes, it does. I know absolutely everything about you." He grabbed my face in his hands and held me still as he glared at me. "I am standing here, *with you*. We have something here and you're tarnishing it. Why?"

"I'm not going to your castle. I'm not a princess." I slapped his hands away. "This was fun but there's nothing more between us. Unless you're here to kill me after all, *Achilles*." He recoiled as if I had slapped him. "I mean, it'd be a good time. I'm not exactly at my best, I'm weakened and vulnerable. Maybe it's your turn to stab me. There's a knife in the drawer. Care to make a play for it?"

"You think that I would do that to you?"

"I don't know. I don't know you. You don't know me either."

He took a step back. He looked me up and down, not with lust this time. It was an assessing look as if to see what my malfunction was. As if something was broken in me and he could find it if he ran some diagnostics.

I wouldn't feel bad about what I was yelling. I couldn't. I would not feel remorse for the hurt in his green eyes.

"What happened, Lea. What changed?" he asked slowly.

"Nothing has changed. I'm still me. You're still you. There's nothing to figure out here. You go back to where you come from, and I go back to..." my voice caught in my throat. "We don't belong together. This was fun. Thanks. Have a swell trip home."

He stood there silent, and still fucking naked and gorgeous. Exactly how all Greek statues were made. I saw my scratch marks on his skin. I saw the scar on his clavicle, and I wanted to touch it because I made it. I had given him those marks. Those were *my* marks on him. His skin was better for having the imperfections I had placed on it.

But castles, and lakes, and countries I would never visit... those weren't real. I would never see them.

"Is that really what you want?" he asked. His face was cold. He had withdrawn himself from me and was now the perfect British man. "To end this before it starts?"

I couldn't say it. I simply nodded.

His shoulders slumped, his head tilted forward. He let out one low, sad growl.

"I'll be on my way." He started to walk away.

I held perfectly still because if I moved even an inch, I'd be clawing into his arms begging him to stay with me.

The further he moved from me, the more my heart sank. Then I heard a hesitation in his step. It was the smallest stutter before his voice washed over me again.

"Make no mistake, Lea," he whispered. "This isn't over. Whenever you're done with whatever you're going through, we will talk about this."

He walked out of the room, the plywood door slamming shut behind him and bouncing off the frame. I heard the rustle of his clothes as he dressed on the other side of that flimsy wall. I listened to his footsteps as they echoed in the cavern of the bunker. His shoes climbed up the metal ladder, to the manhole that loudly scraped open.

It closed again, with a solid, final thud.

I could have stopped him in those long, agonizing minutes.

But I didn't. I couldn't.

A tear slipped down my cheek. Then I felt another. It was minutes–maybe an hour?–before I moved again.

I put on pants and boots, walked out the center console of screens in the main area and opened them up to the cameras we had around our plot of dessert.

There was no sign of him or his car. Müller's car was also gone. Part of Brett's disposal, I was sure.

I wiped the tears from my face, only to feel another come. Another ridiculous, stupid, pathetic tear.

That's enough of that nonsense.

With a deep breath, I tried to relax, clenching and unclenching my fists to get these little emotions out. It was time to move on. So, I busied myself with the monitors.

Callisandra Davenport was on the scene in her khaki shirt with plenty of large pockets. Her microphone was at her lips as the air whipped her curly brown hair around her head. Her crisp British accent came through in that decidedly monotone way: "Tensions are high as reports of the death of the terrorist leader known as 'the Butcher' spreads in the ungoverned space known as Kemet. Baas Medical Tech, the largest corporation to run refugee camps in the area, have started mandatory evacuations of all employees. Officials of the United Nations have voiced their concerns for how the growing violence will affect refugees."

CHAPTER TWENTY-SEVEN

The satellite phone rang, and I picked it up. I was surprised to hear the overhead *ping* of an airport sound system. A multi-language announcement followed.

"I'm not coming home," Leo said without greeting.

"What are you talking about?" I asked, sitting up in the chair. "The mission's done. Come home."

I could hear his ragged voice on the other end. Then he cleared his throat.

"You shouldn't be on this phone out in the open anyway," I whispered harshly. Our satellite phones were supposed to be used in secret, for the quickest, most important communications only.

I could hear him pacing.

"They have her," he finally let out.

"Who?" I had no idea what he was talking about at this point.

"Chloe." He was talking through gritted teeth. "She didn't make it out. They have her. They're holding her for ransom, it's all over the news. I need to go get her."

"What are you talking about?" I was baffled at this point. "Who the fuck is Chloe?"

"Doctor Laurent." That was the pretty doctor. Why was he bringing her up now? "I'm not leaving until I get her."

"What?" I switched my screens to the live streaming news channel. Of course, Callisandra Davenport was there, standing at the Turkish-Kemet border. A picture of Dr. Chloe Laurent was in the corner. The words "kidnapped" and "ransom" were on the ticker tape scrolling underneath.

"I need to get back in there and get her." I heard him take a deep breath. After a moment he asked, "Will you help me?"

This was a bad idea. Getting back in there should be the last thing on his mind.

"Where are you?" I ask.

"Istanbul airport." I could still hear the foot traffic near him. I heard the music on the overhead speakers and the announcements, one right after the other.

"I don't know what you want me to do. You can't go back in there." It was ridiculous. "Her family is just going to pay the ransom and they'll let her go."

"Get your friend to do it. Your Scottish friend," he said angrily into the phone.

"You shouldn't be talking about this out in the open," I hissed at him.

"I don't fucking care!" he shouted. "I need you to get me back in there so I can get her out." He went quiet for just a few seconds while I tried to formulate a response. "I've never asked you for anything. I've done everything to take care of you my whole life. This one time..." He audibly snorted through his nose. "This one time, could you do what *I* need you to and find a way to get back in there."

That was the only thing he could have said that would have given me pause.

He was right. He had never asked me for anything. He was always the giving twin. The Pollux to my Castor. The stronger of the Gemini.

"Okay," I said. I didn't know how I would do it. I didn't know what I could possibly do. But I would figure it out. I had to. Because he asked me to.

He sighed. In that sound was all the world's burdens leaving his body.

"Thank you." He said it so softly that I could barely hear it.

A tear went down my cheek. I don't think he ever really said that to me before. Not with this amount of gratitude or feeling. Why was I crying again? Twice in one day?

I cleared my throat. "Don't forget to eat."

I hung up on him.

I had no idea how to get him into an active conflict zone. That was out of my scope. But I knew someone who would know. I knew someone who had the right contacts, and the right skills to be able to do exactly what my brother needed.

And I kicked him out of my bed.

What would I need to do to ask him for this favor? I looked at my reflection in one of the darkened monitors.

I truly looked at myself and touched my face. I tousled my platinum hair, and ran my fingers over my flat cheeks, and dried lips. With a bit of work, maybe I could help win his favor. He was clearly attracted to me. He wanted me. Would he still want me, after all of this?

CHAPTER TWENTY-EIGHT

Strathlachlan, Scotland

THE COUNTRY HOUSE'S LIBRARY was made of oak and leather-bound books. A lit stone fireplace stood on one side, filling the space with crackling warmth. Leather seats were held together by gold push pins on frames that pre-dated the Americas. The smell of book glue, ash and lingering cigar smoke and whiskey perfumed the dark, academic surroundings.

I normally found that comforting. But not today. Not when an infuriating Atalanta was running from me.

I stared at a map table with a painted replica of Joan Blaeu's world atlas. The countries had been updated to show post WWII countries. The frame had ornate ink and watercolor depictions of the world's gods and prophets interacting from between the clouds and oceans.

This was my first real extravagance after coming to my inheritance. A map, just to remind me how big and connected the entire world was. The map was held in place under a clear resin, and I had drawn on it many times over the years with erasable markers, putting dots in places I had gone, and places I wanted to go. But there was still a blank spot over California, where I left *her*.

I pushed the thought out of my mind to consider a different woman. A woman in distress who needed my help.

On the map table was a tablet that I used to watch the news. Chloe's face, wide-eyed, and scared was staring at a camera as someone yelled for her to speak.

"What is your name?" the voice behind the camera demanded.

"*Doctor* Chloe Laurent." For all the fear she exhibited, she was still defiant. *Good girl, Chloe. Keep that fire, it'll keep you alive.*

In my head, I was changing the mantra – *Chocolate is thicker than blood. Chocolate is thicker than blood* – as I tried to formulate a plan to rescue her.

Kemet wasn't on the map. The ungoverned space didn't exist when it was created. The puzzle of how to get into Kemet – and soon – was weighing on me. I couldn't blend with the locals. I'd have no freedom of movement. I couldn't hide amongst aid workers since most of them evacuated. Options were limited.

We could just pay the ransom, but that was always tricky. No one liked doing that because it meant that there would be more ransoms, and more kidnappings. It would become a business. Paying a ransom had to be a last resort.

A frontal assault was out of the question. I'd need a small army. While the combined wealth of all St. Michael's chocolatiers could pull it off, governments didn't like the existence of private armies. Not even temporary ones. They didn't like knowing that we could raise the type of manpower that could overthrow governments. That was just inviting scrutiny and chaos.

There had to be a solution staring me right in the face. I just needed to find it.

Geordie and I compiled Müller's text messages to the Ferryman prior to Rashid Junior's death. We stacked them with printouts the bank transfers wired into Müller's account as soon as Rashid Junior's death was confirmed.

We bundled that into a folder with the Caledonia Security seal and offered it as proof that Müller was the one behind the assassinations.

I presented it to Rashid Khan myself. Offering my further condolences. I also hoped it would bring him closure now that Müller was dead.

Rashid Khan still grieved for a son. His once black hair had turned gray. He was stepping down from his positions, choosing to retire with his wife. I hoped that their retirement could bring them peace.

"So, it's true then," he said, his voice melting with grief and soft with regret. "Someone killed my boy. For money." He chuckled without humor. "Probably my own flesh and blood too." He turned his head to the side, his cheeks looked sallow in the harsh light. "You were right. If I had left my money to charity, then no one would have had a reason to go after my boy." Then his dark eyes turned to me, and he looked like the weight of the world rested on his shoulders. "You are lucky to not have family. Guard yourself from those who are closest to you."

"I can continue the investigation," I offered. "I can find who ordered the hit and who planted Müller in your security team." I was clutching at straws, looking for anything that could ease his burden. "There could be something else at work here."

I still hadn't told him that his son was involved, that his Swiss accounts had illegal money, and that there was probably more where it came from. He wasn't ready to hear that.

He might *never* be ready to hear that.

"What does it matter?" he said it so dismissively, so coolly that it struck me to the core.

I left Rashid Khan, a God among men, beaten and broken behind his grand desk, like a King who won his throne but lost everything else. All the money in the world would never pay for what he truly wanted.

He formally announced his retirement later that day. Most of his assets would go back into his companies and boards of trustees. What remained of his personal wealth would be given to charities. He even earmarked some towards my own endeavors.

Rashid insisted on transferring the ten million bounty into Caledonia Security's accounts. I told him to keep it, but he insisted. My failure to protect his son, and my lies to protect my woman, led to a profit for my company. I felt dirty about it.

At least she was safe now.

I fought the urge to do more. To place a tracker on her, somehow. Every day, I kept myself from telling Geordie to hack into her phone, her email... to find her on CCTV. I wanted to just see her face, and know she was okay.

I took my eyes from the map when I heard footsteps coming to the door. One side of the large, oak double door opens, and Alastair is there. Tall and slim, with a half-smile on his lips and brow arched up.

"You have a guest," he said, mocking the voice of a snobbish, ancient butler.

"Come off it," I told him, shaking my head.

"Well, you truly do have a guest, *laird* Callum." He poked fun at my title and leaned on the doorframe, one ankle crossed over the other. "Shall I show her in? Or let her know that the lord of the manor is indisposed?"

"Her?" I was shocked. "Chloe? She got out on her own? How?"

"Not Chloe." Alastair pretended to pick some lint off his lapel. "Shall I keep you in suspense? I find this all quite delicious."

"Just tell me already!" I barked. Louder than I meant to.

"Well, she did say, and I quote..." He cleared his throat for dramatic effect, before affecting an American valley girl accent. "Tell him this place is a dump."

My heart stopped. It dropped to my feet.

Alastair turned around and walked away without another word. *It couldn't be...*

I straightened, staring out the small diamond panes of glass that faced the rose garden, marked with stone bird baths and fountains. The sky was gloomy and gray – as it was most of the year – which made the colors of the grass, the trees, the autumn flowers even more vibrant.

There was a moment of silence after Alastair left.

Then light footsteps came from the hallway. I could tell the exact moment she entered the room, her jasmine scent flooding my senses.

"I went to your castle first. The new one, not the old one." Her voice was like a bell, crystal clear and melodic. I shut my eyes and couldn't help the smile that came over my face. I didn't want to turn around. I didn't want to lose whatever spell I was under.

I knew, down to my bones, that she'd be back. It was our fate. She would be mine. But I didn't think that it would happen this soon. Had it been a day? Or an eternity?

"They said you were in your country house." Her slow steps behind me marked her movement. "Your staff were really helpful." She stopped just a foot behind me. I could feel her heat. Her presence. The air she was breathing. "When they said country house, I thought they meant a house in the country. You know, maybe some three-bedroom kind of thing with a carport."

I wanted to turn and grab her. I wanted to wrap her in my arms, but she was a skittish bird. My possessiveness may make her run again. I clenched my hands into fists to control myself.

"Can you tell me something, Lord Callum?"

I didn't like her using my title. It was something she sneered at in disgust. I'd give it up if she wanted me to.

"How the fuck does this monstrosity not count as a castle?"

"There's a very specific reason." I slowly turned to her, not reaching out, taking as little space as possible. Her eyes met mine. "But I don't recall what it is right at that moment."

At the sight of her, I licked my lips. She was glorious in jeans, hiking boots, and sleeveless t-shirt. I could see the contour of her muscles, and she was better than any statue of a goddess that was displayed in the Louvre. Through my awe, I noted that she had color on her lips. Even her eyes had a little liner. Not as much as when she met me at the bar in LA, but it was there. It was subtle.

On her shoulder was a brown leather backpack. I took it from her and placed it on the ground. I could see marks – *my* marks – on her clavicle and neck, which she didn't try to hide. Under that shirt would be the bruises left by my hands.

"Have you come to your senses, lass?" I leaned my forehead down to touch hers. "Are you ready now?"

I couldn't resist anymore. I grabbed her by the scruff, pulled her towards me and kissed her. She threw her arms around my neck and my other arm went to her waist. I pulled her hips to mine so she could feel my hard cock against her. I needed her to know what she did to me.

She pulled her face away. Her eyes scanned down to my throat. She smiled with mischief as she looked back up to me. I quirked my head.

Her hands came to my shirt, and in one violent tug, she ripped it apart, sending buttons skittering across the floor. She stepped away, her eyes raking over my abs with a hunger I hadn't seen before. She bit her lower lip.

"Do you want me to fight you for it?" I growled, stepping closer to her. She stepped away. "Because I will chase. It will be my pleasure to do so." She stepped away again. I stayed still. "I don't think you're ready for what may happen if we do this."

"Aren't I?" she asked playfully. Her hands went to the hem of her shirt, raising it just a little to show the deep grooves of her abs, to the small flat belly button over her belt. My mouth watered. She continued to step away from me, to the other side of the map table.

"You need to stop, love," I warned her. This would be her final warning. "After this, only your safe word will be able to stop me."

She tilted her head, an evil glint in her eye. Her crystal laugh escaped, so perfect, so devious, so ready for me to devour.

"I'll happily open that pandora's box." She pulled the shirt over her head. No bra. Her small breasts were held up by her tight, defined pecs, and her brown nipples were erect and ready for me to suck, pinch, and bite.

I let out a growl. She laughed and turned to run, but I was faster, pouncing on her half naked body and slamming her back to the map table. She tried to squirm out of my grip, grunting with the effort. She planted a boot on the hinge of my hip. I grabbed her ankle and held it in place, stopping her escape and pulling her back to me.

She tried to flip over, her ankle twisting in my hand until her glorious back was exposed to me.

"You know better than to give an enemy your back," I tutted, pulling her until her legs dangling off the table and she was bent at the waist.

"Enemy?" she said, breathlessly. "I thought I was meant to be your lover."

"My lover, my enemy." I bit down on the space between her neck and shoulder, ready to mark her again. "You'll be more and more until I have everything."

I pushed an arm under her, squeezing it between the smooth wooden desk and her breast. It fit beautifully in my hand, and I squeezed it until she whimpered. My cock stiffened at her noises, and I pushed my hips into hers. My Brioni dress pants barely contained me, not when I was aching to be inside her again.

I slid my hand from her breast, down her tight abs, to the button of her denim jeans.

She squirmed, hitching up one leg on the table, ready to try to escape again. She threw an elbow into my ribs, and I grunted at the impact. That would bruise later.

She tried to crawl out from under me, but I grabbed her hair and pulled. Her back arched, she sucked in a breath, then growled in frustration. Her back bent so beautifully, displaying the muscles of her lats, her tiny waist and her ass pushed back against me. One hand in her hair, the other unbuttoned her jeans and started pulling it down until the top of her plump ass was uncovered and exposed.

I pulled her jeans until they slid down to her thighs, restraining them together. Black, plain bikini panties covered her arse and I grabbed it until it ripped from her body. The cloth left red marks on her hips, and I traced it with a gentle finger.

"There are so many ways I want to mark you as mine," I growled.

She moaned, and it was all the consent I needed.

I undid the fly of my pants, pulling out my cock. I slipped the head into the beautiful gap between her firm thighs, to the wet heat that got slicker with every struggle.

"You like this," I said into her ear, putting my weight on her back and pinning her hips further into the ground. "You like the fight. You get wetter the more I trap you, don't you?"

She whimpered, gritting her teeth.

"Answer me," I growled into her ear, pressing my cock into her entrance. Just a little bit. Just enough to feel her squirm and push back, so I knew that she wanted this too.

She whispered a small, resigned, "Yes."

"Good girl." I drove into her waiting cunt. She screamed, her hands planted on the table, and she pushed back into me, wanting more. I groaned, feeling her struggle to get more of me inside her. I kept completely still, pinning her down from inside her pulsing heat.

I wouldn't give her satisfaction until she admitted that she was mine. I needed her to admit it, and I would resort to using her sexual frustration against her if necessary.

"Tell me you're mine." I bit her ear, pulling her hair to emphasize my demand.

"Never," she whimpered and smiled, taunting me.

I pulled out until only my tip was in her wetness and was rewarded with her frustrated whine. I groaned into her neck, smelling that sweet jasmine. I kissed her cheek. She pushed her face into my lips, her hair teasing my skin. She was so exquisitely desperate.

"Tell me you're mine," I repeated.

Her mouth hung open and she shook her head, her brow creased. I eased my cock inside her just an inch or two. Her eyes shuttered closed and she gasped in anticipation. I don't know where I found the strength to stop before seating myself completely, but I did. I pulled back to her entrance and a whine escaped her throat.

"Please," she whispered.

I kissed her cheek again, my hand tracing down from her shoulder, over her breast, to her stomach that quivered with her unsteady breaths.

"One day, you'll beg for me," I whispered to her. "I will *make* you beg."

My hand went further down to her belly button, and lower to her mound and hovering lightly over her swollen clit.

"But today, you will admit you're mine." I swiped her clit and her eyes closed and she whimpered, trying to buck her hips for more. I chuckled at her. "Admit it and I will give you more than you can handle."

She shook her head, but her conviction was melting away. It was glorious. My little goddess was giving away her power.

"Say it!" I growled and she shuddered.

"I'm yours," she whispered, her eyes closing in resignation. She cleared her throat and said with more conviction, "I'm yours."

I closed my eyes and let my head fall into the crook of her neck. My grip on her hair loosened, just for a moment as my cock pulsed with need. My control snapped and with a feral growl I thrust into her while my hands pulled her into me, slamming our bodies together so hard that her hips bounced off me, slamming her into the edge of the table. My hips followed hers until she was pinned, my hand still between her thighs, teasing that little bundle of nerves.

She was on the edge, I could feel it, but I had to make my point clear.

"Say it again," I commanded.

"I'm yours!" she screamed, then followed it with a keening cry as she came, her juices coating my hand and cock. I followed soon after, placing my hands on the table, to keep my weight from her. I slowly moaned as I pulled out of her heat, severing our connection.

I immediately missed the closeness and pulled her up against me, supporting her back against my chest as I felt her legs shake under her weight. She pulled her pants back up to her waist with shaking hands. I embraced her, my hands massaging her breast and her quivering belly.

I ran my fingers from her navel, up her ribs and to her throat and back down again.

"I won't be able to stand much longer," she said softly.

I picked her up bridal style and laid her on a green leather loveseat, placing her head gently on an embroidered pillow. I got to my knees in front of her and stroked her hair.

"That was..." she started to speak but stopped and just smiled contentedly.

"Aye, darling. That was…" I leaned over to her and touched my nose with hers. "… lovely."

Her fingers tightened on the collar of my open, ruined shirt, pulling me closer to her. I kissed her cheek, her nose, then her lips.

"I'm scared to ask but is it always like this for you?" she whispered, nervously. "I mean, before. Have you ever…? Like this? With someone else?"

"Never," I said firmly. I wanted her to have no doubts. "Never outside of my own fantasies have I had anything close to this." I kissed her full on the mouth, devouring her again. When I pulled away, I looked her in the eyes and cupped her face. "You've opened Pandora's box now. Which means that if you pull away from me again, I will come after you."

"Because I'm yours?" she sweetly asked.

"Aye, darling, because you're mine," I chuckled. "Now that I've had this, I need more."

"More? Didn't I satisfy you?"

"I won't be satisfied until I've had you in every room." I leaned down to kiss her throat. "In every field." I kissed her clavicle. "In every glen." I kissed in the valley between her breasts. "And tasted every inch of you." I kissed her right breast. "And memorized every bit…" I kissed her left breast. "Of your golden skin."

I bit at the edge of her ribs, and she gasped and pulled away with a ticklish giggle. I held her hips down and kissed her belly, before laying my cheek just above her navel and making her the warmest pillow. She ran her fingers through my hair.

"Callum?" her soft voice asked.

"Yes, my little goddess," I said, not opening my eyes.

"Goddess?" She laughed. "I like that."

I tilted my head up to look at her through the valley of her breasts. She propped her head on her free arm, looking down at me. Her smile melted away, and she bit her lip. She looked to the side, before dragging her eyes back to me.

"What is it, darling?" I asked her. "Tell me what's on your mind."

Her belly rose and fell beneath my cheek as she took a deep breath. Her trembling hand left my hair and came to my shoulder.

"I-I..." she stuttered. Her hand trailed down to the Rolex watch on my wrist. "I need your help."

I sat up. I rearranged my cock back into my pants and closed my trousers. My heart was pounding in my chest. I looked down at her and tried to keep my voice calm.

"Did you do all of that because you need a favor?" I felt my brogue get thicker with the words. My posh accent was gone, and what was left was me in my rarest form. "Was all of that...pretend? To get me to..."

"No!" She shot up onto her elbows, her breasts thrust up, her brow creased. "God! No! I mean... I liked it. I wanted it. What happened was...but I thought that maybe..."

"You thought that you could throw yourself at me..." I ran a tense hand through my hair, pulling at it from the root. That's why she colored her lips and lined her eyes. This was premeditated. "...and I'd be willing to do something for you."

She swallowed. "Yes, but don't think for one second that I didn't want everything that we just did, and that I didn't mean what I said."

I searched her face for signs of deception but found none.

"I do need your help," she admitted, "but I would have been here sooner or later. Please believe me."

She slipped off the couch and joined me where I knelt on the floor. She placed her hands on my cheeks and kissed me. I recoiled. She pulled back as if I had slapped her.

Then her hands dropped to her sides, and she started to shiver like a leaf. She looked away, her mouth open.

"I... think..." She whispered. "I feel..."

Fuck! I was doing this all wrong.

She was still raw, and vulnerable from what we had done. I should have thought about aftercare, but I hadn't. Now she was quivering and falling apart before my eyes as her adrenaline fell. It was my job to hold her together and I was doing a crap job of it.

I cupped her face and kissed her. She returned that kiss with desperate earnestness. I swallowed her whimper of relief. When I broke the kiss, I brought her head to my chest and pulled her onto my lap.

"Alright, lass," I cooed into her hair. She curled into me, bringing her knees to her chest, her forehead nestled into my neck. "Next time you need something from me, you ask. No tricks, no games. Do you understand?"

"Yes." She was shivering and not from the cold. "I swear."

I pulled her in a little tighter. I felt the relief in her body as the tension eased.

"Do that again, and I'll punish you for it." I promised with a firm kiss to the crown of her hair. "Now, tell me what you need from me, darling."

Lea and Callum's story concludes in **Exposing Adonis**

THE STORY CONTINUES

<u>IRON AND STEEL</u>
Irish Mafia
Iron Rose (Rose and Alastair)
Steel Rain (Ajax and Sinead)
Iron Blade(Eoghan and Kira)
<u>MOURNINGKILL</u>
US Special Forces/Military Romance
Four Calling Birds
Fire for Effect
<u>UNGOVERNED SPACES</u>
Spies, Assassins and Caledonia Security
Exposing Atalanta(Callum and Lea 1)
Exposing Adonis (Callum and Lea 2)
Taming Achilles (Geordie and Pippa)
Tempting Apollo (Leo and Chloe)
Unleash Hades (Hugo and Cali)
Come join me at Thorny Tales, the facebook group, for give aways and general shenanigans.

I frequently do giveaways on my newsletter at MollyBriar.com